ONE-NIGHT STAND

ONE-NIGHT STAND

SIMON TAYLOR

LARRIKIN House
www.larrikinhouse.com

Larrikin House
An imprint of Learning Discovery Pty Ltd
142–144 Frankston Dandenong Rd, Dandenong South Victoria 3175 Australia
www.larrikinhouse.com

First published in Australia by Larrikin House 2021 (www.larrikinhouse.com)

Written by: Simon Taylor
Cover designed by: Anna McGregor www.annamcgregor.com.au

A CIP catalogue record for this book is available from the National Library of Australia. http://catalogue.nla.gov.au

ISBN: 9780648894506 (paper back)
ISBN: 9780648894544 (ebook)

FORESTFRIENDLY

NATIONAL LIBRARY OF AUSTRALIA

A catalogue record for this book is available from the National Library of Australia

To the younger me.

Don’t do it.

The characters in this novel are fictional.
Any likeness to comedians or normal people is
intentionally coincidental.

1

'NOW, PUT YOUR HANDS TOGETHER for the hilarious Ben Thomas!'

The audience at the Exford Hotel consisted of three teenaged-looking backpackers and a greying man asleep on the front-row couch. When the MC, Mick Allen, announced my name I was on a barstool with a nervous leg bouncing on the footrest. My hand was holding a text message from Tash. I'd read over it four times since she sent it a minute ago and it made me oblivious to my call to the stage.

'Ben.' A fellow comic, Libby Davis, nudged me and flicked her head sideways. 'You're up.'

I slid off the barstool while trying to put my phone away. It slipped from my fingers so I kicked at it to fend it from the drop. It rebounded off the side of my dirty sneaker and hit the wooden floor. The thud was louder than any of the four or five claps from the crowd. Well, 'crowd' was optimistic. The failed phone-saving manoeuvre put me off balance, I fell backwards onto the stool, knocking it to the floor as well. Libby helped me up, shaking her head and smirking as the backpackers turned to see what was going on.

'Let's try that again,' Mick said. 'Ladies and gentlemen, please put your hands together for this idiot, Ben Thomas!'

I jogged to the stage past the hopeful number of chairs the staff had put out. When stepping up, I was careful not to trip and further delay the show no one was begging to see. Mick passed me the microphone since the stand had collapsed during the first act. He left the stage, muttering something unintelligible yet loud enough to make his irritation known. He found a seat at the bar and ordered a beer with a lazy attempt at a whisper.

'Thank you, keep it going for Mick Allen everyone,' I said. The clapping had stopped a decade ago. All I received was a forced 'woo' from one of the four comics at the back of the room.

'I um.' The text message made the phone feel heavier in my pocket. It pulled focus away from my rehearsed jokes. 'I'm trying to work out what kind of man I am.'

I studied the room, as if it might help. Despite convention, there were no spotlights to create a warm glow around the performer and a comfortable darkness over the audience. The Exford Hotel avoided these pleasures by only having sharp fluorescent house lights, bright enough to illuminate the blank stares on the backpackers' cheerless sunburnt faces.

'I think there are two kinds of men. There are manly men and there are flamboyant men. I think I'm a bit of both. I'm caught between, "I want to build my own house one day" and "These curtains look fabulous!"'

I was meant to flop my hand out like a glamorous interior decorator to sell the punchline but my nerves restrained me. It came out instead as a weak shrug. The backpackers smiled a bit but it wasn't enough to ease the brutal chasm of silence. I could have been doing the gig from space and heard the same response.

The sleeping man up the front made a single snore.

'This guy gets it,' I said, pointing at my biggest fan. The comedians at the back spat out laughs. The backpackers only offered bewildered faces.

'Comedians like it when another comedian is dying,' I tried to explain. The comics kept chuckling but it still didn't register with the teens.

I ran my fingers along my eyebrows so I could cover my face for a moment. It was hard to tell where the backpackers were from. Maybe English was their second language and I could blame my bombing on a linguistic barrier.

'Where you guys from?' I asked.

'The UK,' one of the girls said, making the sad state of the room all my fault.

'Sweet,' I said and paused to nod in silence. My comedy brain tried to find a reference to the UK. *The Queen?* No that's lame. *Brexit?* Overdone. *Fish and chips?* Get the fuck out of here. The expiry date on a witty comment had long passed now and my voice made the clunky tone change a comedian does when they return to rehearsed material.

'Anyway, I haven't always been a performer,' I continued as if the game we had all agreed to play was to pretend this was a credible comedy gig. 'I was actually a carpenter. For two days.'

One of the backpackers puffed out through his nose. The comedians had gone quiet again. Libby put gun fingers to her temple and pulled the trigger. My heart was thumping louder as the silence in the room grew longer. I tried to swallow but even my tongue had lost faith in me. The woman behind the bar was now using her phone, her eyes lit by the cool blue light like she was heading towards a tunnel to a better life.

'The problem with being a tradesman is that my bosses kept trying to get me to do weird things that I'm not used to. Like work.' I paused again. A laugh was meant to go here. It felt like when you're walking down stairs, expecting an extra step but instead you land on the floor with a jolt of your knee. Unpleasant and jarring.

At least there was a sense of shared discomfort. I didn't want to hog it all.

'They'd ask me to hang a plasterboard and I'd just say "Nah, I might just do a Bachelor of Arts."'

The blonde backpacker girl coughed and then began to chew her hair.

A long, loud sigh left me. Just to stave the silence off for a moment longer. A few of the comics spluttered out sadistic laughs. Those arse-holes. My focus was being sapped by the urge to leave and read over Tash's message again. I stared at my feet. They were on the precipice of a steep fall to my comedy death. I could back away to embarrassment or jump forward into humiliation. My phone felt heavier and heavier.

'About a month ago,' I said, 'I had a one-night stand.'

One of the backpackers, a dude in a vomit-yellow beanie, let out a supportive grunt. He looked like the guy you would see police arresting out the front of a pub at 3 a.m. The tattoo on his neck poked up out of his collar just enough to scare off old ladies and reputable employment. His reaction kept me talking, though pending felons weren't quite my target audience.

'And tonight,' I went on, 'I got a message from the woman telling me she is pregnant.'

A few people gasped. The room was awake now. The blonde backpacker whispered something to her friend while keeping her eyes on me. The comics were murmuring to each other now too. The woman behind the bar looked up from her blue screen.

'I don't know how to feel. I'm not ready to raise a kid. I don't have a house because my parents are still alive.'

The sleeping man stirred but only enough to indicate he was in a nightmare too. The pain in my gut from reading Tash's message intensified. Guilt and shame were sharp emotions when you had to digest them.

'When I got the message,' I said, 'I realised I need to go buy nappies. Not for the kid, *I'm* shitting myself.'

I grabbed at the microphone stand to finish the set, then remembered it was broken and left it against the red brick wall. There hadn't been a laugh yet.

'This is real, by the way. This is happening right now. I haven't even told my family. Just you guys. You're my family now. We're going to get through this together.'

There was a noise from the back. It was either a comedian, or a mouse, or the sound an existential crisis makes when entering a room. The backpackers were still there, which was reason enough for any comedian to keep talking. I'd seen performers bomb for ten minutes and win the audience back right at the end. As long as the ship hadn't sunk, you could turn it around. In theory. Though tonight could be the exception.

'So, I didn't wear a condom.' Boos came from the whole room. 'But! But to be fair, neither did she.'

The female backpackers groaned and squirmed in their seats.

'Come on!' I continued, 'I was an idiot. I was in my twenties. I still am, so I don't know what that says. But look, it's easy to get a false sense of security when you're young. You think, "I can't get an STD, I'm in my twenties! I have pure skin! I wash with Nivea!"'

The groans had gone but they hadn't been replaced by any sounds of approval.

'Hey, I was just amazed I was even having sex. Look at me. I look like The Hobbit in skinny jeans. I look like… I look like the head of Wolverine on the body of a skeleton.'

The blonde teenager pushed her face into her hands. I'm not sure what expression she was hiding but I guessed I would agree with the sentiment. Beanie guy was staring, his mouth half-open. He had a tattoo of a Pikachu on his neck yet still had the gall to look judgemental.

'So when I met this girl I just… I don't know, I just went with it. I didn't have a condom. What kind of arrogant prick walks around ready for protected sex at any moment? I mean, you don't walk around with a saddle just in case you find a horse to ride. That's not the best analogy but you get what I mean.'

My head was cocked towards the floor now, hoping a hole might open up so I could fall through onto the ground floor and make an escape. I willed the stage to consume me and spit me out into freedom. It didn't listen though. Like the rest of the room, it was just embarrassed for me.

'And who wants to spend all that time getting out a condom, then putting it on, then using it, then taking it off, then tying it up, then flinging it across the room and then forgetting to pick it up in the morning? Not this guy. I'm trying to reduce the use of plastics in this society. Have you ever watched a nature documentary? When I'm about to have sex I'm thinking of turtles forced to wear little condoms hats. Can we please stop killing the environment with safe sex practices!?'

There was no response to warrant me continuing. The comedians at the back perched like wolves ready to tear me up for not getting a single laugh. Tash's message awaited my reply. The audience awaited the end of my set. The barwoman appeared to be waiting to tell the general manager that perhaps a comedy night wasn't such a good idea after all.

'Also, it wasn't my decision alone, by the way. The girl and I spoke about it at length. I remember the conversation in full:

'"I should get a condom."

'"I'm on the pill."

'"Sweet."

'That was it. But I think it's clear we're both to blame.'

The blonde backpacker made a disapproving noise as she crossed her arms.

'Yes, I know. I know. It was stupid not to use protection. However, I wasn't reckless. I'll put this in the most delicate way possible: I didn't use a condom, but I didn't…' My eyes squeezed shut. 'I didn't send the "troops" in. I deployed them on a neighbouring region.'

More groans.

'I was just following orders! That's the etiquette as far as I've ever learned. The guy announces the oncoming ejaculation and the woman directs him as to where to put it.

'The guy says he's about to finish and then the lady says…' I heightened my voice, '"Finish inside me!" or "Do it on my stomach!" or "Cum on the lava lamp!"'

The vomit beanie guy laughed hard. I don't think he was following what was going on but he heard the word 'cum' so that must have won him over. It was enough to create an exit, though. The laugh, however cheap, was a portal back off stage and I intended to dive through it before testing the limits of self-torture.

The middle-aged man on the front couch woke up. His groggy eyes appeared bloodshot as he shuffled himself around in the seat. He wiped at a drop of spit that had pooled from his mouth while sleeping. I sighed.

'Sorry,' he mumbled.

'Don't be,' I said. 'I'm jealous of you.'

Libby chuckled. Not much though. My phone vibrated.

'Anyway, I'm Ben Thomas. Have a good night.' Two of the backpackers made a few forced claps before Mick lumbered to the stage. I fumbled the mic into his outstretched hand and walked off the gallows to a freedom I didn't deserve.

'Ben Thomas, everyone!' he said, to no accolade. 'Wear a condom, you dickhead!'

The man up front erupted in violent laughter. Would have been nice earlier.

At the back of the room, I grabbed my phone from my pocket while the other comics grinned like devils. The screen yelled at me. A call was coming in. From Tash.

2

FOUR WEEKS AGO, I was doing gigs in Perth. It's a beautiful city when the sun is setting over the river and you can't be anywhere else. Enough money from the recent mining boom had come to pave every road anew. In town, the windows hadn't collected more than a speck of dust and you could still smell the paint on a park bench. Perth was too young to be strutting around with all these expensive arts centres, sculptures and theatres. It was like seeing a facelift on a toddler. The city had the spoils of affluence but had never grown the personality to match it.

Great beaches though.

My friend Jin was letting me stay at his apartment. He's that guy at parties that everyone says should do comedy but really shouldn't. Being funny in conversation doesn't always translate to holding court on stage and Jin proved it. He was too buff to need more attention, anyway. His wardrobe was full of v-neck shirts and his cupboards were stacked with vials of chemicals that made his muscles grow beyond their genetic recommendation. If you were close enough to him, you'd know what fake tan and testosterone smelled like together.

Jin had started doing open mic rooms about six months ago. Seeing him die on stage was a cheap thrill. He'd have a decent set one night and then forget what he had said by the next one. The spark was there but he couldn't keep the fire going long enough to justify doing comedy full-time. Stand-up requires hard work and discipline, both of which his parents in Malaysia had ensured he never developed by sending him money every week. He had a big screen TV in both his living room and bedroom and a sneaker collection that warranted its own apartment. It included a rare pair of Jordans that he'd never taken out of the box. His fridge was filled with food still in delivery bags. Jin would order a chicken kebab with chips and a salad, get impatient, have a snack and then neglect to eat the original meal. More of that local affluence.

We were in his living room one Friday night, about to head out. The TV was playing some real estate show for the Baby Boomers who were staying in for the evening. I had my skinny black jeans on and my only pair of sneakers: scuffed white Cons with a hole forming at the toe. I used Jin's cologne because I never bought that stuff. My hair smelled tropical from doing my special trick of putting a dab of conditioner in it instead of hair gel. My style was thrift.

Jin was standing in the kitchen area rubbing bronze lotion on his arms as he finished a story about a music festival he'd been to over the Christmas holidays.

'So yeah, police dogs were at the front of the festival entrance,' he said. 'Bro, I had like three grams of weed in my pocket. I ate the whole bag before I went in. Then someone told me the dogs only smell for pills and shit. Man, I wasted all that weed for nothing.'

'You should do that story on stage,' I said.

'Nah, I don't want people to know I'm a dealer.'

'Mate, I'm pretty sure the bum bag is a dead giveaway.'

He huffed, his pecs flexing through his shirt. 'I never carry weed in my bag. That goes in my shoe. Oi, let's get out of here.' He fished out a dexi from a white pill bottle, popped it in his mouth, then washed it down with a swig from a near-empty bottle of vodka on the kitchen bench. A 'dexi' is what some call Dexedrine. It's used to manage symptoms of ADHD. Jin doesn't have ADHD but he knows a guy, who knows a guy, who knows a guy who does. That guy buys them legit and sells them to whoever pushes enough cash his way. People like Jin use dexis for a kind of recreational focus.

Jin had put more chemicals in his body than a pharmacy could stock in a warehouse.

Once, Jin had almost been arrested when trying to post human growth hormone from Thailand to himself. He wasn't trying to sell it, he claims, he was just buying in bulk to maintain his hot gym bod while saving money on postal fees. The dexis had made him very organised.

This was the third night in a row Jin and I had ventured into the Perth nightlife. This featured bars full of men with muscles too big for their shirts and women with tans too orange to see their shoulder tattoos. The main pastime at these places was drinking to the point of altercation. Twelve beers into a conversation meant it was time for a fist to the temple. You'd see muscle lords holding their friend back from charging at a stranger, while their girlfriends made high pitch noises for ambience. The federal government was spending hundreds of thousands of dollars on ad campaigns to stop people from 'coward punching' each other and I bet this city got a fair slice of the budget.

We went to a fistful of bars crammed with tradesmen and miners sipping away their hard-earned pay. They made crazy money doing FIFO work: Fly In, Fly Out. A miner might do two weeks of intense work on site and then take two weeks off to drink everything. I'd met twenty-year-olds in Perth with a forklift licence who owned more bright yellow utes than I had socks. These guys were buffer than me, richer than me and rougher than me. If aliens ever came down to Earth and separated the species for their intergalactic zoo, I wouldn't be in the same cage as the Perth boys.

At Rosie O'Grady's in Northbridge, an Irish pub too full to contain any comfort, Jin and I lined up at the bar. We turned our sights to a rabble of buff boys who were standing nearby, chanting with their fists pumping the air. They were all at least six foot apiece, with boulder shoulders and assorted patterns inked into their forearms. One of them stood in the centre of the ruckus, drinking beer from a shoe. Inspecting his feet confirmed the expected. Yep. His own shoe.

The man drained his suede boot as the v-necks around him cheered. Jin laughed and whooped along with them. These were every guy that bullied me in high school. Abrasive without effort. They'd have the hottest girlfriends and the coldest demeanours. Their natural talents on the sporting field would breed bravado in every other aspect of their lives. When they passed you in the hallway they'd slap you on the back of the neck just because fuck you. It was just a joke! Get it? You don't get it? Well then fuck you. I'd never felt comfortable in a room with guys like that and now I was in a city full of them.

'That was awesome!' Jin said, his jaw hanging open so that his chewing gum was visible on his bleached white teeth.

'Dude, I don't mean to be an arsehole but can we go somewhere a bit less hectic?' I asked.

'In Perth?' Jin bent an eyebrow at me. Even his forehead had more muscles than normal. My sagging shoulder communicated all the exasperation I wouldn't be able to yell above the noise.

'Literally anywhere we don't have to deal with dickheads doing shoeys,' I said.

Jin moved his jaw sideways a few times.

'Okay,' he said. 'I know somewhere.'

* * *

The Court was Perth's biggest gay nightclub. It's only one, I think, but it doesn't sound as good when your claim to fame is 'no other option'. Neither Jin nor I are gay, despite what was yelled at us from the Nissan Skyline that rumbled down the road.

The building stood like a peacock on the corner of a main road, rainbows painted all over it. Under the flamboyant paint job, it was built like a classic pub. We went inside. The upstairs had been decorated like a laser-light wet dream. Slick black tiles lined the bar above polished wooden floors. Purple lighting was held in the air by the haze of a smoke machine. White spirals spun around the room, criss-crossing with green lasers and disco ball reflections.

The dance floor welcomed me while Jin lined up at the bar, bumping his head to the thick pulsing bass. There were a lot of topless men with shaved chests but none of them were drinking out of their shoes: otherwise known as gentlemen.

I spun and clapped along with the sway around me. Dance moves for straight men are so limited when you have a narrow definition of masculinity. These moves include: *step-step-hold-a-beer* and *aggressive-pigeon-neck*. In a gay club, you were free to parade your jazz hands, spirit fingers and supermodel struts – all the stuff you can tell that tradesmen are suppressing beneath their macho exteriors. By the time they are drunk enough to attempt these moves, they are too intoxicated to achieve them.

A woman danced towards me. A real human woman. She had a blonde bob haircut and a face. What a face. Her purple lipstick matched her bra, visible under a translucent white shirt. The glitter on her eyelids sparkled under the pulsing lights. Her skin was fair except for a brush of red on each cheek. She laughed at my chicken-like stride and then impersonated me on the chequered dance floor, her hair bouncing as she moved.

I scanned for onlookers to see if I'd get in trouble. Not that being there was against any rules, but trying to pick up a straight woman at a gay club was like bringing your own steak to a vegan restaurant. The gay community has fought social, cultural and political battles to be recognised, respected and accepted, this was their place to have fun, without the influx of a bunch of arseholes hitting on women who are otherwise unencumbered by the relentless propositions they could expect in regular bars and clubs. I did *not* want to be one of those arseholes.

But what a face.

Her glittered eyes fluttered as we danced towards and away from each other, back and forth. We rolled our bodies and pointed our fingers in the air. We stepped in close to shake our shoulders and then pulled away for spins. A guy with platinum blond hair came past us and yanked the buttons of my shirt open on his way to the bar. It made me laugh. I started to rebutton but my sparkling dance partner pulled my hands away and ran her fingers across my bare chest. It tickled but I wore a tough face.

Without a flicker of warning, she stepped in and pressed her purple lips to mine. When we pulled away, she giggled at the lipstick mark she'd left on me. With my fingers under her chin, I guided her back to a kiss. Her arms found their way over my shoulders, locking me into her heat. Strange hands pried us apart. The platinum blond had his mouth wide open and his eyebrows tilted in faux rage.

'Oh my god, get out!' he said.

We both giggled at him and I raised my palm in apology. I snatched up the purple-lipped lady's hand and scurried off the dance floor to a corner of the room. With my forearm on the wall, I leaned into her ear. I'd seen John Travolta stand like this in the movies and I needed to borrow some cool.

'What's your name?' My voice made it just above the thick electronica. Her perfume had the sweet smell of cocktail cherries.

'Ash,' she yelled back.

'Ash?' I checked.

'TASH!'

'Tash. Cool! I'm Ben. Want to go talk?'

'I want to go home,' she said.

My arm melted off the wall. I buttoned my shirt back up to no protest.

'You can come,' Tash clarified when she saw my defeat.

Oh. Sweet.

'Oh. Sweet,' I said.

She clasped my hand this time and led me towards the stairs. Jin was still at the bar. He looked at me as I waved goodbye and then glanced over at Tash. His confusion turned into a sly grin. He made a gun sign at me and clicked his tongue. I crossed my fingers and smiled back.

Downstairs, the street lamps glowed as the busy road hummed with people arriving to begin their night. Tash said goodbye to a man standing outside smoking, then hailed a cab that had just dropped people off. She held the rear door open for me with a grand wave of her arm.

'Ladies first,' she said, laughing at her own joke.

'Why thank you, sir.' I put my hand over my heart and bowed before dropping my bum onto the back seat. She joined me and pushed up close.

'Where you heading?' The driver didn't turn around.

'Fifty-nine Queens Crescent, Mt Lawley,' Tash said to him. She leaned on my shoulder with both hands and whispered through giggles into my ear.

'To have sex.'

No response from me. Words can change minds. My palms were sweating so I rubbed them on my jeans. There had to be something wrong with her. Maybe she was a murderer. Maybe she was one of the guys from the Irish pub wearing a mask who was about to tear it off and do a shoey. She might be a social justice warrior who goes to gay nightclubs to kidnap straight men who hang around the place trying to pick up ladies. How did she know I was straight?

'How'd you know I'm straight?' I asked.

'Because straight guys stare at my boobs,' she stated like a scientist. 'Gay guys just grab them.'

'In that case,' I grinned, 'I'm totally gay.'

* * *

We made for her bedroom, throwing our clothes off before we even hit the mattress. Tash took her bra off, while I yanked at my jeans. They got caught on my heel so she pulled my hands away and removed them herself. I looked her over. Her undies befit a Victoria's Secret poster. Not that I've ever stared at one for too long. I'm just pretty observant. My undies were whatever had been on top of my suitcase that morning.

Stripped of our wrappers, Tash seized the back of my head by my hair and pulled me towards her. She kept changing position and pushing me around to where I would be most useful. She told me to kiss this and touch that and go here and squeeze there. I was just happy to be involved.

After an hour of rolling across her sheets, her body succumbed to a wave of twitches and trembles before she breathed a long soft exhale. Mine had done the same a bit earlier but I stayed in the game to be a team player.

When we flopped away from each other, panting, I lay on my back and stared up at the ceiling. In the dark I couldn't see much, but her room smelled like candy. Her breath slowed to a calm lull as her body grew still. I peeked sideways at the silhouette of her nakedness and smiled.

Gay clubs are awesome.

***

In the daylight, I could see Tash curled up on the other side of the bed with the sheets pulled up to her chin. They were pink with little flowers on them. On the wall above her bed, she had fairy lights strung between the shelves, which were cluttered with framed photos of her and friends. Piles of gold jewellery and coloured stones were scattered between books. The spine of one of them read, *The Woman I Wanted to Be*, well-worn with a bookmark halfway through. Under that was *The Sartorialist*, *#Girlboss* and *The Chiffon Trenches: A Memoir.* None of them had been made into movies so it was going to be hard to relate.

I rummaged through the sheets to find my undies, trying not to disturb her. The rest of my clothes were at the foot of her bed. Attempting to slide into my jeans in silence made me lose my balance. I fell against the cabinet, smashing my elbow into the drawer. I steadied myself but my leg was still caught and I fell backwards onto the carpet. My skull made a hollow thud on the flood. I bit my tongue to stop every swear word from escaping all at once.

Tash groaned as she began to turn. I froze. She went still again.

Teeth clenched, I pulled my pants on, trying not to move too much. They settled around my hips without a sound from Tash but then I zipped up the fly.

'Why are you on the floor?' Tash lifted her face off the bed enough to see me.

I stood up.

'I was trying not to wake you.'

'Well done.' She dropped her head back to the pillow.

'So, uh.' I found my shirt and put it on. 'Should I um.' I hesitated again. 'Can I get your number?'

'I'm asleep,' she groaned. There was no replying to that so she continued. 'Where do you live?'

'I'm staying in the city but I'm actually from Melbourne.'

'Why bother then?'

'Ouch,' I said.

She rolled over to face me. We'd manage to remove most of the purple lipstick from her mouth over the course of the night. I rubbed at my cheeks, assuming I now wore some of it as face paint.

'Fine.' Tash found my phone on her bedside table. I told her my passcode and she added herself to my Facebook. Her full name was Natasha Peters. Her profile photo showed her at a music festival wearing a flower tiara and making peace signs with both hands.

'Do you want to get breakfast before I fly out today?' I asked as a gamble. There was a clear enough vibe for me to guess the answer.

'I want to sleep,' she said, closing her eyes and pulling a pillow over her forehead. I paused. There was nothing left in the room for me except dejection.

'It was nice to meet you.' I forced a smile in case she looked up.

Her head lifted off the bed so that I could see the glitter around her eyes again. Some of it had migrated to her cheeks, forehead and ears. She squinted at me and scrunched her faded-purple lips.

'You're short,' she said.

'Well this has been great, thank you.'

Tash dropped her face to the pillow once more and either fell asleep or pretended to.

***

I thought that was the last time I would see that face.

It now appeared in a little circle on my screen, demanding I answer the call. A video call? This was escalating. I could let it ring out. I could throw it across the room. Instead, I dashed down the stairs of The Exford Hotel and into the Melbourne streets. The air was cold but my skin was already covered in goosebumps.

'Hey, I'm just walking home, how about I call you a bit later?' I said, trying to dodge other pedestrians. She brushed her cheek with her white knuckles. There were rub marks under her eyes in red streaks. She was on her bed with the fairy lights behind her, but they were off. No glitter tonight. She wasn't looking at the screen as she spoke.

'I want to keep it.'

3

'I DON'T UNDERSTAND WHY you can't just let me do this on my own,' Tash said from the video feed, propped against my desk lamp. The phone speaker crackled. 'You don't need to be part of it.'

If she hadn't understood at 1 a.m., she wouldn't understand at 6 a.m., but my fingers wouldn't hang up. I was either going to get through to her or die of sleep deprivation. Either would be welcome at this point. My eyelids were hanging over my pupils and my mouth drooped open. I'd needed to pee since the gig at The Exford but given we couldn't reach a resolution, I was hoping my bladder would just explode and take me with it.

'Because,' I said, jerking my head back up, 'I will be a part of it. You think the kid is going to grow up never asking where dad is? I'd feel like a piece of shit knowing I had a kid out there I wasn't looking after.'

'But I'm giving you an out,' she said. 'I'm fully capable of raising a kid. I've got savings, plus I can get support from my parents when I tell them. This wasn't part of my plan either, Ben. But I can still make my life work with a child in it.'

'Tash, I keep telling you that it's not that simple for me. I have a career. But I'm not making enough money to pay for my gas bill let alone support a kid. I would be such a shit father if I tried to keep it up. That's why I'm saying, if you have this kid, my career is over.'

'Career' was hyperbole. My sister Penny once described what I do as a 'hobby I sometimes get paid for'. Jobs with early-set alarms and peak-hour traffic were features of purgatory to me. The creature comforts for a comic starting out were scarce, but if you were funny enough, the rise up the ranks would be swift and you'd be rich and famous on television. Maybe. This conversation with Tash wasn't the screen time I'd been shooting for. I was already too far into comedy to quit but not far enough in to tell if I'd ever make it. It was this cycle of doubt and optimism that kept me rolling forward.

'I'm not trying to guilt you,' she said. 'I'm just telling you what I intend to do and you make the decision that's right for you. You can go about your comedy career, I'm fine with that. Or move to Perth for the kid if you have to.'

'Perth!?' If the camera had been wide enough to capture them, Tash would have seen my arms fly up. 'There is only one comedy club there, right, so that's one week of work per year. Maybe two. The rest of the time I could do the mining tour but that's only a few weeks of work. Then what? All the TV stuff is in Sydney and Melbourne. Flights back and forth would be a nightmare. If I want to provide for a kid I'm better off working behind a bar than I am trying to keep up a career from the other side of the fucking country.'

Tash's mouth was gaping during most of my rant. She was only waiting for me to stop talking.

'And I'm saying,' she said, 'for the millionth time tonight, that you don't have to give up your career. I'll raise the kid. You can…'

'Be a piece of shit? Is that it?'

'That's your choice.' She leaned back. A single lock of hair poked up from where she had been tugging at it all night. 'I won't judge you for it.'

'But can you see the two options you're giving me?' I said. 'I can be an arsehole or drop my career. I just don't see why you want to bring a kid into a fucked situation.'

'I'm not making it fucked, you're making it fucked,' she said.

'I'm not doing anything, I'm just telling you what the situation is.'

The cityscape of Melbourne stretched across the horizon, visible from my bedroom window. The sun was rising through a pink sky. It brought a soft blush to my surroundings. My eyes began to sing as the light intensified. The blinds had been broken when I moved in a year ago. I was meant to ask the real estate agent to ask the landlord to get them fixed. I'd since got used to the discomfort and the effort seemed more painful than the original problem. My forearm shielded my eyes from the light but the sting remained. 'I don't even know why we're still having this conversation. It's clear you've already made a decision.'

'Ben, I'm not trying to ruin your life,' she whispered.

'Well, you're not ruining it. It's just not the right time for me to have a kid.'

She was ruining it.

I'd always had my life planned out in order: get famous, buy a house, get a dog, use that dog to attract a girlfriend, get married, have kids, and then gaze into the sunset while the hopeful music from *Star Wars* played in the distance. This surprise baby was blocking my vision into a perfect future. Now I had *no idea* when I would get a dog. And would I even get famous if I was spending all my money buying nappies? And all my time changing nappies? And all my energy hating Perth? Famous people didn't have to deal with that stuff. They had a personal assistant to handle their surprise pregnancies and emotional meltdowns.

I was scared of Perth, too. I'd had three near-death experiences there. Once, I was crossing the road when a cab hit me. My body slammed onto the pavement. A gruff, old driver wound his window down only to say, 'Oh. Ah. Shit,' and then drove off. If I hadn't been concentrating on my phone while crossing the road, I'd still be mad. It took me a couple of days to see a doctor. My chest got so painful that I overdrew my savings account to pay a GP to tell me I had broken two ribs. He said I was lucky I hadn't suffered a punctured lung. I told him I was relieved because with one lung I'd only be able to tell half my jokes. He let out more of a cough than a laugh.

I spoke to Tash through defeat. 'If you're keeping it no matter what I think, then just say so.' I wanted to collapse into a deep sleep for at least the next eighteen years and nine months. My body would have to survive on the bits of dust that landed in my mouth when I breathed. There would be plenty to eat in this apartment.

Tash left the chair she had been sitting on and migrated to the floor with her back leaning against the side of her unmade bed. She tucked her knees up to her chin and rested her cheek on them. If she was trying to hide her beauty with poor posture, she'd picked the wrong form.

Perhaps it was just the low resolution of the video feed but there was a softness to her features that made it hard to believe she could be so stubborn.

'I don't know what to tell you anymore. I better go.' She reached up to her screen.

'Wait, wait,' I shot a look down the barrel of the camera. 'Be honest, okay? Pretend like I'm not involved at all. Would you consider… Okay, this sounds so harsh, but…' I paused to find a way around a word I didn't want to use. 'Do you think you could ever go through with not keeping it?'

Tash closed her eyes. She exhaled.

'No, Ben. I know myself. I'm having this child.'

The words bounced around space for a few seconds too long before echoing out the speaker. It felt like thunder despite how quiet it came.

'Okay.' I nodded. 'Okay.' A wave of tears welled up from my toes, pushed through my body and splashed out my eyes. They were heavy down my face and I didn't want Tash to see. I tilted the phone away so the camera only caught the wall.

'Hello?' she asked, but I couldn't speak. 'Are you there?'

I wasn't. I was at a funeral for the life I had always wanted. The open casket presented my dream lying stiff and cold before me. It was so young. It only had me to send it off into the afterlife. My wet eyelids closed as I mourned for it in silence. Goodbye sweet chance at fame. So long you Lamborghini that I would drive into the Sydney Opera House car park for a sold-out show. Farewell magazine cover with my Spanish supermodel wife and three kids in front of our Byron Bay mansion. You were so close to having it all until you let your lusty little balls ruin your pending success. You poor fool.

'Fine.' Tash ended the call.

The walls stood around not saying anything. They knew I was too upset to respond right now. My wallet sat on my bedside table, skinny and sad like its owner. It must have seen my longing stare because it broke the silence to say, 'I can't help you, dude.' My room consisted of a black metal bed frame, a mattress from my childhood bed, my red fixed-wheel bike, a faded bedside table, a dilapidated wooden desk the previous tenant had left and a red desk chair on wheels that squeaked when they rolled. Every object around me looked uncomfortable. They had heard me talk about money and feared they'd end up in an op-shop. There wasn't anything I could sell to afford a baby, anyway. Nothing of mine, at least. My *Seinfeld* DVD box set was the most expensive thing I owned. Nine seasons of observations and social faux pas on a disk that was already obsolete technology. The episodes were timeless but streaming services had ruined my ability to provide for my pending offspring.

I went to the bathroom to ease one of the thousand pains in my body. Nine hundred and ninety-nine to go. I flushed the toilet and envied the water that got to escape into a world of less shit than I was in. Sobs came. Shallow breaths darted in and out of my crooked mouth. My legs moved me to the front door, picking up speed and desperation as I swung it open and bolted downstairs. The Melbourne air tackled me with its sharp chill despite the present sun. My arms flailed as I ran past houses that stood gasping at me. The suburb turned into the city, steel blue buildings bouncing the sounds of morning traffic off each other.

The footpath became busy with suits and corporate skirts avoiding me as I bolted across the pavement at a pace inconsistent with safety.

The Yarra River, brown and lazy, glimmered just enough to draw me towards it. I ran along the path where a surrounding parade of Nike shorts and Adidas runners made me aware of my jeans and collared shirt, that were reluctant to absorb my streaming sweat. My feet slammed harder to the concrete to pull my attention to a lesser agony than the thought of paternal obligation. My knees almost creaked under the impact. My toes were swearing at me, asking me to stop. Still I ran, off the path now, away from the growling freeway above and closer to the water. Under a bridge, overgrown grass slowed me down until I had to balance myself just to move forward. There were no other idiots so far off the running path. Mud licked at my shoes and slid me towards the water. Before a misstep, I came to the gaping mouth of a mammoth drain on the side of the hill, sloping down to the river. Graffiti covered the surface of the concrete opening. The stillness of the cavern entrance offered refuge.

In the darkness, a slender stream of water led me forward under the grey slabs that curved overhead. Generations of spray paint coloured the slabs in patches of warped letters. The further in I got, the fewer there were. My pace slowed as the blackness accumulated around me. There was just enough light from outside to reveal thin black letters sprayed high above me: 'The Cave Clan Welcomes You'. My foot stepped on something. Crunch. There was a scream from below.

'Oi, fuck off!' yelled a voice.

A squeal left my mouth. Not one suited to my age. The high-pitched noise ricocheted through the concrete cave. If I hadn't been to the toilet already I would have filled my jeans with fear. Death shoved its sickle into my behind and I bolted for the entrance. Before darting back, I stole a glimpse of the grimy bearded man. He had revealed himself under a grey blanket just to yell at me for squashing his foot. I don't know if he was part of the Cave Clan but he sure hadn't made me feel welcome.

I sprinted to the light, tasted the breeze, leapt over the fence and pushed my way up the hill until a stitch poked at my guts. At the top, the main road was filled with potential witnesses for any murderer following me. My adrenaline soon left me with only sweat and embarrassment. I limped along the footpath until realising this was Richmond and changed direction. There was a side street with its sign missing. Halfway down stood a red brick apartment with a half-dead shrub out front. The gate was jammed so I thrusted my shoulder into it a few times. It popped open with the promise of leaving a bruise on my upper arm. The bell had never worked so I banged on the frame of the screen door.

'Hello?' I yelled. No reply. 'Hello!? Libby? It's Ben.'

A minute tested my patience before a sliver opened up behind the mesh of the screen door.

'What are you doing here?' Libby's voice was raspy and either confused or annoyed.

'I…' I suppressed a sob. 'I think I'm actually going to be a dad.'

She opened the inside door enough to reveal her silhouette through the mesh.

'Woah. So that set was true?'

'Yeah,' I said.

Libby shook her head. 'Mick didn't believe it, he thought you were just trying to get a rise out of everyone.'

'I just spoke to her and she's keeping it.'

'Good for her,' Libby said.

'Yeah, for her.'

'Don't be an arsehole, Ben. You don't know what it's like to be pregnant.'

'I know, I know.' I dropped my head and closed my eyes for a beat. 'I'm just not ready for a kid.'

Libby opened the screen door. Strands of her red hair blew off her face before she pulled me in for a hug. I didn't return it. Instead, I just let her arms squeeze around mine. She rubbed my shoulders and then put her hand on my stomach.

'You're not showing yet,' she said.

'Fuck you,' I said through a broken grin. She enjoyed my reaction.

'I'd invite you in but Dane is still asleep.' Libby flicked her head towards the bedroom.

'It's okay. I better get home.'

'And have a shower,' she wrinkled her nose.

'Thanks for bringing that up.' I smelled my shirt and then took a step back to avoid any more ridicule.

'I need one too now.' She sniffed at her dressing gown. 'So, what are you going to do?'

'Have a shower,' I said.

'About the kid, you idiot.'

My shoulders shrugged through fatigue. 'I don't know. Head to Perth maybe.'

'Perth? Jesus, is that where she is?' Libby scrunched her face tighter than she had at my smell.

'Yeah.' I pinched the skin between my eyebrows. It helped me avoid seeing whatever expression she was making now.

'It could be worse,' she said. 'You could be broke.'

She was even more pleased with that one.

4

I ROLLED OUT OF THE foetal position, off my bed and onto the carpet, then curled back up into the foetal position. Another twenty-something minutes went by before I groaned and tried to stretch out the aches. Most of them stayed. I yanked my bed sheets until my phone fell out and landed on the carpet. One eye was open just enough to see the screen and start a call on loudspeaker.

'Hello?' Dad enquired.

'Hi, Dad.' My neck felt swollen from the inside.

'Ben?'

'Yes, Father.' If it was too much to ask of him to save my number in his phone, he could at least try to remember his son's voice.

'You home all day?' I asked.

'I am. Just been doing some gardening. I bought a new soil that I wanted to try. It's been pretty rainy the last few days. We had about three mil on Saturday, which will be good for the—'

'Alright, I'll see you soon,' I cut him off to save having to plug my phone into the charger. He could talk the life out of a battery. 'You can tell me all about it when I get there.'

'Alright, see you soon.'

'Wait Dad, is Penny around?' I asked.

'No, why?'

'No reason. I'll see you soon.'

Penny had moved out before me, but visited Dad more often. She somehow managed to find the time despite her superior and all-important corporate career. At Christmas lunches with the extended family, she'd sit with folded arms as the relatives fawned over me being a comedian. Every year they'd say variations of, 'That must be so hard!' or, 'It must be so rewarding'. Penny would sometimes throw out soft retorts like, 'Not financially'. I'd recline in false modesty, waving away the notion that being a full-time comedian was some thankless, esteemed role in society. The praise gave me a satisfaction Penny couldn't buy with her income as a whatever-the-hell-she-was. It was a thin satisfaction though. If she had been at Dad's right now, I wouldn't go. Her witnessing me ask Dad for money was a punch to the ego I wanted to dodge.

Dad spends most of his time listening to talk-back radio and huffing to himself while reading news articles about the latest political scandal. From the day he retired, refusing to spend a cent had become his life's work. He'd even taken to selling off old furniture once he'd worked out how to use Gumtree. A few months ago, he called me up to come give him a haircut because, 'I'm not paying thirty-five dollars for something I can get you to do for free!' He since learned that I lacked the patience and steadiness with the clippers. Now, Penny cuts his hair because he'd rather risk incompetence again than pay for a guaranteed acceptable haircut.

There were no clean socks left in my drawer so my runners went on raw. I collected my bike and left. My arms and legs had now given way to orders from my stomach. If I couldn't get a dollar from Dad, I could at least visit his fridge.

* * *

I pushed open the door to Dad's place to find him in the hallway holding an empty glass with the rim towards wall. He had a piece of paper in his other hand. He was moving the glass towards a huntsman spider, which crawled a few centimetres away from me as I entered. Rude.

'Got a new friend there, Dad?'

'I do. Leave the door open, I'm going to put him outside.'

Dad placed the glass over the eight-legged creeper with a gentle hand. He glided the paper under it and stepped out into the front yard. I held the handle to keep the door from blowing shut in his face, as this wasn't the setting for classic slapstick comedy. When he returned he gave me a hug hello. I wanted to hold on and collapse onto him. Instead, I stiffened up and gifted him a gentle pat on the shoulder blade.

'Your mother would have made me kill it,' Dad said.

He'd bring her up like that sometimes. Even the smallest of moments would be tied to a memory of her. One time last year he was walking Penny to her car and choked up just because he thought she walked kind of the same as Mum.

'So, what do you need?' he asked.

'What do I need? Just wanted to come say hi.' My eyes inspected the walls for any hidden lie detectors. The framed photos hanging up seemed dustier today. Images of Mum and Dad had faded to a sepia tone. Penny featured in only a few of them, one wearing denim overalls and a backwards vaporwave cap. She looked disapproving, even as a child.

'What are you up to?' I asked.

'I was going to hang the tarp out back if you wanted to give me a hand.'

'Not really.' I said.

'Not really, hey?' His hands went to his hips.

'Fine. Let's go,' I tugged the door closed and plodded towards the back of the house. 'But I'll leave any spiders I find for you.'

I made a detour to the kitchen to raid the biscuit shelf. I shoved six chocolate wafers into my mouth and took a gulp of milk, holding the bottle an inch from my lips. I combed through the fridge fast in case Dad came back inside to hurry me up. It was stacked with packets of premade meals like 'slow-cooked lamb shanks' and 'chargrilled steak'. I could smuggle one into my bag before the ride home.

In the backyard, Dad had bags of manure strewn all over the large red garden tiles. I'd helped him lay the tiles a few years ago. You could tell which ones I had placed by their liberal estimations of alignment. This further represented Dad's philosophy of 'why pay a professional when you can botch a job yourself?'

A triangular green sheet lay across the wooden outdoor table with clumsy holes cut in the corners. A series of odd strings and ropes were tied through them, each salvaged from a different era in his life. The ropes might have been from a camping trip we took two decades ago, the strings could have been from his shoelaces from the third grade. He'd store them until he needed them or archaeologists dug them up.

'You know where the ladder is?' Dad asked.

'Yes, Father,' I said, trudging over to the garage past more odd ropes tangled like piles of spaghetti. The ladder was on a shelf above a mess even a hoarder would gasp at. There were rusty tools, saggy mattresses, yellowing books, unused exercise equipment, bikes that hadn't been ridden in a decade, and every other object that has ever existed. A dusty dartboard hung upside down on the wall with a dart still in it. I plucked the dart off, stepped back, almost tripping on a white crate, then threw it with all my strength. The dart fizzled through the air and punctured a hole in the tin wall of the garage. Perfect.

I pulled the ladder down from the shelf but misjudged my ladder-pulling-down abilities. My heel clipped the side of the crate and the ladder fell sideways despite my attempt to steady it. The legs of the ladder ploughed straight into the dartboard and ripped it off the wall. Perfect.

After recovering from the crash landing, I left the dartboard to be dealt with by someone who cared and lugged the ladder out to Dad.

'What took you so long?' he asked.

'I got distracted by your treasure trove.'

'Alright, I'll hold it in place, you climb up and tie the end of the tarp rope to that hook up there.'

I climbed up with one hand and held the rope in the other. Three rungs from the top I stopped and leaned against the wall. My cheek pressed against the cold brick while I struggled to thread the frayed end of the rope through the hook. The hook appeared to be about as secure as I felt.

'How old were you when you had Penny?' I said.

'Hm, twenty-eight. Don't tie the knot just yet.' Dad said.

'What?'

'Don't tie the knot until I adjust the tarp.'

'Oh, right.' I held the rope in place while Dad made sure the tarp would reach the other hooks. 'Do you think you were ready to be a father when it happened?'

'You work it out as you go along. Tie it on now,' he said.

The only knot I knew was through-the-loop-and-hope-it-works. It seemed to hold, but I didn't test it too much.

'Why you asking?' he said.

'Just wondering.'

'Hmm.' Dad put his hand on my back as I climbed down off the ladder. 'I think I made some mistakes.'

'Really? Like what?' I asked.

'I didn't teach you how to tie a knot properly.' Dad went up the ladder and re-tied my work. When he stepped down, he turned to me and ruffled my hair.

'But besides that,' he smiled, 'you turned out okay, didn't you?'

'Ha'. I couldn't smile back. 'I suppose.' It wouldn't be long until he found out about all the mess I'd made. Both in the garage and my life.

'Alright,' he said, 'do the other rope now.'

'You're better at it than me, I'll hold the ladder.'

My phone rang with Tash's name.

'Hold on, Dad. I'll be back in a sec.'

He pouted as much as a man his age was allowed to.

I hurried down the hall far enough away to discuss a crisis in frantic peace.

'Hello?' I said, scurrying into my childhood room and kicking the door closed behind me.

'I fucked up,' Tash said.

'What?'

'I just spoke to the doctor…' Before her next words came, my phone slipped out of my hand and landed somewhere behind the old wooden desk. I stretched out on all fours to retrieve it. My arms began to shake; chocolate wafers weren't conducive to upper body strength. My middle-finger flicked at the corner of the phone until it hopped back into my grasp.

'Wait, Tash. Sorry. I dropped the phone. What did you just say?'

'Oh god, don't make me say it again.'

'Say what again?' I asked.

'Jesus, this is embarrassing.' Tash forced a cough before dripping the words out between hesitation. 'I spoke to the doctor and the date of the pregnancy is… not what I thought.'

'Okay.' I didn't have a follow up question. Tash exhaled hard enough to push me over through the phone.

'I slept with another guy about a week after you. So the baby could be yours… or it could be his.'

My arm gave out from under me. My head and phone both made thumps. Tash's voice was gone so I checked my phone screen. The battery was dead.

'Fuck!' I said, for all the reasons.

In the backyard, Dad was dragging another tarp towards the ladder. He was too busy to hear a long, confusing explanation of a situation I didn't even understand yet. Instead, I asked him a pressing existential question.

'Dad, do you have an iPhone charger?'

'I don't think so,' he said.

'Okay, I've gotta go home. Something came up.'

'Wait, we haven't finished the tarps!'

I was inside and on my way to the front door quick enough to pretend I hadn't heard him.

5

'SO THE MENSTRUAL CYCLE is confusing.'

Chuckles greeted me from the dark theatre. The spotlights at Crown Casino lit the stage, hot enough to cook a fly from a distance. I twisted the mic off the stand. It was heavy but cordless so if I wanted to, I could stride across the stage, feeling loose and free, or vulnerable and unhinged. It would depend on how this went.

'I don't understand the menstrual cycle at all. As far as I know, it's like the Wheel of Fortune down there. Every month you spin the wheel and it eventually lands on "egg". I'm not a doctor.'

The whole crowd wasn't with me but enough of them were to stop me running out of the theatre and diving out the window into the Yarra. My skin went from desert to swampland and I loosened my grip on the microphone to stop it popping out of my hand and hitting me in the teeth. That had happened once before, by the way. It got a big laugh at the time but the impact chipped half of my front tooth clean off. Over a week went by before I could get it repaired. The dentist didn't understand how I could squeeze a microphone so hard it projected into my mouth – she obviously didn't know anything about the pressures of comedy.

'I went to an all-boys school so we didn't listen in sex ed. I'm sure the teacher was saying things like "These are the ovaries, the fallopian tubes, the uterus…" but the only thing that registered in our horny boy brains was "VAGINA". That's all I can remember about sex education, "VAGINA, VAGINA, VAGINA! YEAH!"'

I mimed high fiving a fellow student with a big dumb grin on my face. If the crowd knew what was behind that grin I could be nominated for an Oscar. Before coming on stage I'd paced around the dressing room, checking my phone every few seconds in case I missed its beep. Tash was meant to have visited her doctor and updated me, but needling her about it only created more bickering. Each day of waiting withered my nervous system further into a husk.

To compound my hidden meltdown, the big comedy agents from A-List were in tonight. Every year they run a showcase to see the up-coming talent and consider who to sign to their roster. I got the gig because of the TV spot I did last year. I got that spot because I knew a guy who worked on the show. I knew that guy because we did a musical together in high school. I did that musical because I wanted to get out of doing sport. My avoidance of physical competition had landed me in the arts industry. At this point, I wasn't sure if I was a talented stand-up or a just terrible everything-else.

'They need to teach sex education like maths. You know, rather than just give you the theory they should give you problems to solve. Like: if a train leaves the station travelling at thirty kilometres per hour, and a second train leaves the same station travelling in the same direction at forty kilometres per hour, how far from the station was the first train overtaken by the second train? And if you sleep with a woman on that train without a condom, what are the odds you need to pay child support?'

The bit was too wordy but some of the audience got it.

'There are so many things I didn't know about sex until recently. For example, I didn't know if you could get someone pregnant from pre-cum.'

'Yes you can!' A woman's voice bounded from the back of the room. The audience gave her a cheer and laughed.

'Well, madam,' I replied, 'I looked it up online and discovered that there is actually a fierce debate on this topic between science… and *Cosmopolitan Magazine*.'

My laugh was bigger. Thank god.

'And by the looks of it, those two can't seem to agree on anything! But here's the best information I can find: pre-cum is made in a separate gland to sperm. So there is inherently no sperm in pre-cum. However! If you've already ejaculated that day, and by "you" I mean the fellas in the room, not you, madam. If you've already ejaculated that day, sperm can stay in the urethra, that's a fancy word for "dick hole", madam. Yes, sperm can stay in the urethra for hours and hours, so pre-cum can wash it through.'

The crowd gave me silence. I grinned.

'What I'm saying is, you can't get pregnant from pre-cum but you *can* get pregnant from previous-cum.'

That broke it. The laughter wrapped around me like a hug. I leaned into it.

'So what you have to ask yourself, fellas, if you want to know if you've ever had sperm in your pre-cum is this: *Did I masturbate that day?* If you don't remember, well then you'll have to check your browser history.' I could just make out a few younger members of the audience laughing a lot harder than everyone else. Some people let the laughs move their bodies around the seat. A comedian could see it in slight sways in pockets of the crowd. Spectators might even turn to each other for recognition or push the shoulder of someone who the gag related to most.

Tonight there was a row of young guys in the front. The tallest of the pack was getting pushed every which way by his surrounding mates. They all wore letterman jackets, tight over their broad shoulders; the type of guys at school that would make fun of me for doing drama but were too upper-class to become tradesmen. They'd end up as cosmetic surgeons or lawyers for bloated banks and oil companies.

'I masturbate a lot,' I went on. 'For different reasons. Sometimes it's because I'm stressed. Other times it's because I have a morning boner. Or a night boner. Or an afternoon boner. There's a boner for every occasion. Sometimes I masturbate just because I have time to. I'm sure there's an evolutionary reason for it but I haven't done the research. I'm too busy masturbating.'

The lettermen jackets laughed hardest. Relatable comedy.

'There is so much I didn't know until recently. So much! For example, I had no idea that sperm can last up to five days inside the fallopian tubes! What are they doing in there? Get out!'

I relinquished the mic stand now and waved my arm around in the direction of the guys up front, like I was spreading magical blame dust all over them.

'This is typical male behaviour: hanging around longer than you're welcome. Take a hint, sperm. Get out of there! If I had known this when I was younger, I would've carried condoms in every pocket and tucked a few in my socks just to be safe. Hell, I want to give out free condoms to every young person I meet with the warning "Don't let sperm get away! They're good at camping!"'

The letterman boys rocked back and forth, chests pumping with hardy laughs. I liked the term 'killing' that stand-ups used to describe doing well. It felt true when you were so in control of a crowd's breathing.

'Even if you do wear a condom, fellas, you need to know that they are still not a hundred percent effective. Condoms have a two percent failure rate, if you use them correctly!'

I smiled and laughed with the crowd but my stomach hurt again. This was all belated knowledge. It was getting me laughs now but it could have got me out of a lot of trouble weeks ago.

'I can feel the panic in the room. *There's a wrong way to use condoms!?* Yes, my friends. According to my desperate Google searches, there are many. You have to ask questions like: Did you open the packet with your teeth and puncture it? Was the condom expired? Was it too big? Was it too small? Did you wear it?'

It was the first time the whole crowd howled. I don't know how taking heroin feels but someone once described it to me as an internal hug: a thick embrace of your insides that warms your bones. This response from the crowd was vibrating, airborne heroin. It dulled the spikes in my nerves and made me need the next hit.

'You can't just *have* a condom. You can't just leave it in your pocket and hope it radiates protection. You need to put it on!'

My pacing around the stage gave the laughter time to play out. You're meant to stay in the routine, not acknowledge how well you're doing. Jerry Seinfeld said that in an interview once. I'd stored this golden information away for these moments. *Stay in the routine, Ben. Don't blow your load again.*

'Everything you search online about pregnancy will tell you the same thing: "Yes, you can." Can you get someone pregnant if you pull out? "Yes, you can." Can you get someone pregnant if you wear a condom? "Yes, you can." Can you get someone pregnant if they are on the pill and the IUD and the copper coil and the Implanon and you wear a condom and you're in another room just having a cup of tea? "Yes you can!" Don't take any risks!'

The swaying of bodies spread like ripples over the auditorium. The applause began to swell. I tried to guess where the A-List agents might be. Everything beyond the front row was just a silhouette, so it was more of a directional guess. I played to the back of the room.

'Some people even think that abstinence is a hundred percent effective in preventing pregnancy. But let me ask you this, Crown Casino, have you ever heard of a little book called *The Bible*? It contains the *one* case in history where even virginity didn't prevent pregnancy. I think it would have played out like this…'

I popped my hip out and rested my hand on it with a bent wrist. My impersonation of a woman was as terrible as it needed to be for comic effect. Though, I always felt some pang of guilt for the stereotype.

MARY: 'Joseph, I need to let you know that I am pregnant.'

I puffed up my chest and dropped the tone of my voice to an even worse impression of an alpha male.

JOSEPH: 'You cheated!? Mary, how could you? I just paid for our holiday to Bethlehem.'

MARY: 'No, no. I didn't sleep with anyone!'

JOSEPH: 'It's that prick from the stables, isn't it? I knew he had his eye on you.'

MARY: 'Joseph, I swear. It just happened.'

JOSEPH: 'But how can you get pregnant if you didn't do the sex on someone?'

MARY: 'You don't know anything about the menstrual cycle, do you?'

JOSEPH: 'What's the menstrual cycle?'

MARY: 'Yeah, typical.'

JOSEPH: 'Oh, this is my fault now?'

MARY: 'Well, maybe if you got a proper education instead of going to Jerusalem TAFE.'

JOSEPH: 'That's a low blow, Mary.'

MARY: 'Look, I don't know how I got pregnant but these things happen. It must be a gift from God.'

JOSEPH: 'Does the gift have a return policy?'

MARY: 'Oh, Jesus Christ.'

JOSEPH: '… that's a nice name.'

MARY: 'That *is* a nice name!'

'The end!'

I bowed. The audience made all the noises I dreamt to hear and the mic clicked back onto the stand. I ran my tongue over my teeth. They were all there this time.

'I'm Ben Thomas, have a good night!' A wave of noise carried me off stage and landed me in the wings of the theatre. Days of tension fell through my shoulders and out my toes. I dropped to my knees and cupped my face. It felt like thick tears were trying to force their way out but none came. My adrenaline evaporated.

'One more time for Ben Thomas! Now for your next comedian…' The MC's voice faded. I took in a long suck of air, dusted off my knees and walked into the green room like a normal guy with no soul-crippling dread. Mirrors lined the walls, with rows of light bulbs around every edge. The room was empty save for a tall guy in a purple sports jacket standing over a cage of pigeons. I sauntered in, shoving my hands in my back pockets to hide the residual shakes.

'What's up, buddy? I'm Todd,' he said in a bright American accent. He placed a pigeon wrapped in a sock inside his jacket pocket and then extended his hand. His stage name was Todd Power and he lived up to every letter of it: teeth as white as bathroom tiles and hair gelled to spike up in eight different directions like a modern art piece. His tie had sparkling black sequins shining off it. The light caught it like a disco ball.

'Hey, yeah I saw you're headlining tonight.' I shook his hand. It didn't feel like it had any pigeon diseases on it. Though magicians were good at hiding things.

'Yeah, A-List brought me over from LA. This is my first Australian tour. Fun right? I caught some of your set. Really funny, buddy.'

'Thanks. Yeah, hopefully the agents liked it,' I responded to my reflection in his teeth.

'Dude, you were great. You ever been to LA?'

I didn't get a chance to reply. The stage manager strode into the room. His headset clamped to his ears with a microphone jutting out towards his mouth.

'Todd, this is your two-minute call.'

'You got it. I'll come side of stage now.' Todd felt around inside his jacket pocket for a moment.

'Nice to meet you, buddy,' he said to me, 'I have to bounce right after my set. I'm doing a private gig for the president.'

'Wait, you mean the prime minister?' I asked.

'That's the one. Australian politics, huh? Anyway, you on Facebook?'

'Yeah, just search Ben Thomas.'

'You got it, my man.' He took his hand out of his pocket and wiped bird poo off it with a hanky. Our handshake had been just in time. The stage manager escorted him out of the room. I heard a few muffled chirps as they left. It was comforting to know I wasn't the only creature in showbiz that felt suffocated.

***

When I got home I assumed my usual existence on the red chair in front of the laptop. It was 12:30 a.m. I brought up Facebook to see if Todd had added me yet. He hadn't. I refreshed the screen a few times until my brain demanded variation. I clicked open a new message and typed 'Natasha' in the address section.

'Hey, I know we said we need to wait for the ultrasound but I just wanted to ask another question. Did the other guy send the troops in?' I hit send. I stared at the conversation box until the text underneath my message popped up 'seen'. No reply. Trembles came back to my hands. I needed to wee but I didn't move from the chair. The dotted bubble appeared, showing Tash was writing back.

'What does that mean?' she said.

'Did the other guy use any protection?'

'He wore a condom.'

Fuck. It's me. Maybe.

'Did he open the packet with his teeth?' I asked.

'Fuck, Ben. I don't know. It was late. We were drunk.'

It's not me. Maybe.

'Okay, okay,' I said. 'It's all good. Let me know if you need anything.'

'I need to see my doctor. I'll let you know what she says next Wednesday.'

I consulted my calendar. That was over a trillion years away.

'Cool, cool.' I wrote.

Tash didn't reply. The message didn't even get marked as 'seen'.

I crawled into bed and hugged a pillow. My shadow lingered on the bedroom wall, as I had neglected to turn the lamp off. *If I didn't wear a condom and the other guy did, that makes me way more likely to be the father.* I got back up and double checked the Wikipedia page on contraception, then slumped back onto the bed. *Unless he didn't use the condom properly.* Back to the laptop to search again, then back to bed. *Unless I didn't withdraw properly.* This time I reached for my phone and Googled the failure rates of pulling out once more, then dropped the phone onto the bed sheets.

Unless, the other guy was lying.

I looked at my phone again but didn't have anything to search.

The word 'unless' sat on a merry-go-round until sleep forced itself over me.

I tried to accept that there were no answers yet. Just a conception I couldn't explain.

Jesus Christ.

6

ULTRASOUND DAY BECAME THE most anticipated event in my life since I believed Santa was behind Christmas.

As a kid, just thinking about unwrapping a PlayStation or a Super Soaker 2000 would give me a knot in my stomach. What if I didn't get what I wanted? What kind of fractured existence would await me if my desires were left unfulfilled? Oh the drama. In the lead up to Ultrasound Day, I grew a dozen new stomachs and knotted every one of them twice over.

The first day of waiting built the foundation for my obsessive behaviour to flourish.

I was in bed. Classic me. The smell of dirty shirts and dried milk lay over me like an extra blanket. Weeks' worth of clothes, unwashed cereal bowls, crumpled up paper and electronic cables decorated the bedroom floor. A dozen used tissues were scattered beneath a plastic bag hanging from the wardrobe door. The bag was meant to be used as a bin but instead was more of a general target to throw my anxiety at.

I kept Googling the odds of conceiving without a condom over and over, trying to find the one article that just said, 'It's not you, man, relax.' I'd read through virtual reams of random pregnancy forums, filled with pages of people having meltdowns about their own surprise conceptions. Distressed young women in similar situations to Tash were pleading for any help with working out who was the father of their unanticipated child. Most of the responses were 'see a doctor' or 'get an ultrasound dating' or 'lol'.

The ultrasound dating was meant to tell you how old the foetus was based on its size. From that you could determine when conception took place and, in my case, pinpoint who the perpetrator was. I mean the father. The internet really could solve your problems if you were desperate enough to sift through it.

On day two I generated a drop of productivity.

I woke up, tightened my body into a ball and wrapped the sheets tighter around me. A good start. The blinds were pulled down so that the 2 p.m. sun couldn't judge me. My foot twitched as each potential outcome sped around my imagination. Lying still made me dizzy to the point I had to sit up and find my notepad. A few joke ideas made it to the paper:

- Pee on stick
- Ultrasounds for baby submarines
- Finding out gender vs finding out intelligence

That was the extent of my creative surge. There was no point writing the full jokes out longhand until I had a crowd to try them on. In fact, if the jokes worked I wouldn't need to write them out at all. Comedians don't forget lines that get big laughs. 'Pee on a stick' was enough to prompt me to remember what I'd thought up: *When women think they're pregnant they have to pee on a stick. Hopefully one that tells them if they're pregnant. Not just a tree branch.*

That was more than enough work for the day. And week.

On day three I took up watching *The Office* on Netflix. The American one. The crux of the sitcom is that Michael Scott can be an effective boss or he can try to be everyone's friend but he can never do both without catastrophe. Despite being in charge of the branch, having worked hard to get to that position, he has the least control over anything. Including his own life. Relatable comedy.

Almost all successful sitcoms have a duality like this. In *Everybody Loves Raymond*, Ray can either please his mother to get delicious cooking or please his wife to get sex. Never both. In *Scrubs* the main character JD, a young doctor in a teaching hospital, can get his mentor's approval but only if he stops his desperate pursuit of it and focuses on just being a competent doctor. The ultimate is *Seinfeld.* The four main characters in this comedy masterpiece can be true to themselves or fit into society. Never, ever both. My favourite episode is when Jerry Seinfeld finds a near-perfect relationship with a stunning and sweet woman. You could believe this will be a home run for our boy, Jerry. Unless, of course, you know how much of a germaphobe he is. It's all over when you see Jerry's horrified face as he realises his new lady has used a toothbrush that she didn't know fell in the toilet. He can't be Jerry and live a normal, happy life.

Real life was never laid out with such sitcom simplicity.

By the seventh day, I perfected my frantic dance between browser tabs. I revisited every website, forum, journal article, blog post and Twitter feed that even mentioned conception odds. Episodes of *The Office* fit in between. After the finale episode, dread paid me a visit. That son of a bitch. It seems that you can polish off a whole television series in one emotional breakdown. I needed another light sitcom or hard drugs.

My phone went off. I swept it up with a trembling hand and had to enter the code a second time because the first had been such a rushed mess.

'The ultrasound says I'm seven weeks pregnant,' Tash wrote.

I navigated to my calendar app, fingers still shaking. One, two, three, four, five, six… seven. I slept with her fewer than seven weeks ago. Five weeks and three days, I counted. *So it's not me.* But the other guy was a week after me. *So it is me.* But the time frame was off by so much. Acceptance and denial chased each other in circles. *Can it be wrong? Holy shit, I'm the dad. But can it be wrong? I'm going to be a dad. Ultrasounds aren't always accurate right? Oh shit, I'm going to have to live in Perth.*

I called Tash on speakerphone so I could tuck my cold, white fingers under my armpits.

She answered after too many rings.

'So what does this mean? Is it me?' I asked, my voice vibrating like my hands.

'I don't know. I'm confused now. I think it's you,' she said. 'Maybe the ultrasound is just off by a little bit.'

'Right, but it would have to be off by a week and a half. Did you ask your doctor who's more likely?'

'Um.' Tash faltered for a moment and then dropped her voice. 'I didn't tell her there are two possible fathers.'

My anger almost made me vomit.

'What? She's your doctor!'

'Don't yell at me!' she said.

'Sorry. I'm sorry.' I sighted my laptop and flipped the screen open. 'Let me just look it up.'

Tash made noises in the form of words but my search absorbed me. 'Can ultrasound dating be wrong?'. Most results were from community forums. None had any authority other than personal experiences. 'Mine was wrong by four days' was followed by 'I had one that was off by over a week!'. It wasn't a place for medical answers, more just maternal one-upmanship. I stopped reading before I found someone who claimed their pregnancy dating was off by a whole generation.

'Hello? Ben?' Tash checked.

'Sorry, I'm here. I was just trying to get answers.'

'We can't be one hundred percent sure until we do a paternity test. I'm not going to guess based on the ultrasound,' Tash said.

I took the phone off speaker and pressed it to my face so hard I could feel the tendons in my ear compress under the glass.

'Then what was the point of telling me the ultrasound dating in the first place? Can't we do any tests before the kid is born to see who the dad is?'

'I'm not a fucking doctor, Ben. I don't know but I'm not ready to tell my doctor the whole situation. It's embarrassing. So you can wait for a paternity test when the kid is born or you can just bail like you obviously want to.'

'Hey, that's not fair,' I said.

'It's not fair on me either.'

'I know, I know.' I sighed. Fairness was a long-missed luxury at this point. 'Okay, let's just try get more information and maybe consider asking your doctor directly.'

'Don't you think I've thought of that already? It's not easy.' Her voice ebbed away under sobs.

'I'm being an arsehole.' My words softened. 'I'm being a real arsehole.'

Tash didn't say anything. Refuting my claim would have been nice but she was too busy hyperventilating. Modern phones sometimes filter out quieter sounds in the background to give the voices more clarity. The line cut in and out, trying to recognise sounds that were loud enough. Our connection was tenuous in all its forms.

'It's going to be okay. It's going to be okay.' I said it twice – one for each of us. 'I'm not going to bail on you. I'm going to make sure I do right by you. I promise.'

Her crying was beginning to slow and her breath became more regular.

'Are you just saying that?' she said.

'I'm not. I wouldn't even bother asking about all this ultrasound stuff if I didn't care.'

'You care about you.' The words hit me with a thud.

'Hey, hey don't do that," I said. 'I'm… I'm trying to accept that life might be about to change. Neither of us expected this.' Sitcom drama never lasted this long. There had to be a joke much sooner. The characters only argued to create enough tension for a punchline. Ours wasn't coming.

'Hm,' she said.

'So can you just keep me updated?'

Silence.

'Tash?'

'Fine.'

'Okay, alright. I… alright. I'll let you go. Um, let's speak when you know more.'

She hung up. It took a lot of strength not to take my phone and swallow it. Instead, I funnelled my energy into yelling at the desk.

It didn't respond.

***

Another search for ultrasound dating seemed apt. It would have been useful if I'd Googled 'medical degree' and had completed that first. There were websites dedicated to 'pregnancy calculators', which at first I thought helped you calculate how much debt you'd be in when you had the baby. These seemed to be for predicting the delivery date, but could also be used to calculate the foetus progress. The strangest part was, it wasn't asking for the ultrasound dating. It was asking for the last menstrual period… I searched for what that meant, understood nothing and then began to message Tash again.

'Hey, sorry if this is personal but I'm just trying to understand everything. When was your last period?' I reread the message about eight times. My finger hovered over the send button. It felt like the equivalent of asking, 'Hey, sorry to bother you but how often do you poop?'. But I had to know.

I sent it. Not the poop thing.

Tash responded straight away.

'Why do you have to know that? I was on the pill so I have no idea.'

I didn't answer. Upsetting Tash any more wouldn't be good for the baby's health. Or hers. Or mine.

On the pregnancy calculator search page, there were countless websites with more information than I could scan with any precision. They all asked for the last period as a way of determining how far along the development was.

One website, to my rescue, had a drop-down menu with the following options: *due date*, *last period*, *IVF date* and the island in a stormy sea: *ultrasound dating*.

Click.

It showed me a calendar and asked me to enter when the ultrasound was taken and the pregnancy dating it gave. Double-checking I got the dates right, I double-checked again. Then did another double-check. Fifteen more double-checks later I clicked 'CALCULATE' and straightened my posture as if I was expecting a court verdict. The screen flickered to a page of results.

> Estimated due date is 22/1/2018 +/- 4 days by sonogram
>
> Date of conception 1/5/2017
>
> Gestational age today is 7 week(s), 0 day(s)

So it's not me. Oh wait, sperm can last up to five days so it is me. Oh wait, it's just as close to the other guy. Oh wait, I still have no fucking idea.

I sat in my red chair and tucked my knees to my chest. My front teeth chomped at a sore that had appeared on my inner lip. Every time I tried to stop chewing, I'd get distracted by the thought of who could help me and found myself biting down even harder. I needed a medical professional. A free one.

There was a guy I knew from school who became a doctor. His name was Zack Robinson but I'd always called him Zack Snobinson. In my head. He had been the captain of the cricket team but walked around like that title meant he was the prime minister. He'd push in line at the tuck shop and not even look guilty. Drama nerds like me would protest but there was always enough sporting devotees around to allow such a crime. Once, I let him borrow a pen during maths and he chewed the top of it before returning it misshapen and wet. He also might have dated a girl I had been in love with since primary school and therefore crushed my fragile heart with jealousy. But, you know, whatever.

I dropped my feet to the floor and air-humped the chair closer to the desk. The wheels screeched in sync. I found Zack's Facebook page. Even in a profile picture his cockiness was visible. I drafted a direct message.

'Hi Zack, long time no see! Can I ask you a medical question? Nothing serious. Well, it's serious but not life-threatening. Well, not my life.'

Select all. Delete.

'Sup Robbo! How ya bloody going, mate? How's your backswing? Still smashing sixes? Cricket is great. Anyway, can I ask you for medical advice?'

I started over.

'Hey Zack, how you going? I was recently told I was going to be a father, then told I might not be the father, then I was given an ultrasound dating that I don't understand. Sorry to bombard you with this but I'm freaking out and I need someone to clear it all up for me. Here's my number…'

I pressed send before I could reconsider.

For the next three hours I just kept pacing around my apartment, back and forth between the fridge and my phone. Neither had anything for me, no matter how many times I checked. At one point I tried to pick another sitcom to watch but none of the characters could act like a bigger idiot than I felt.

Finally my phone rang.

'Zack?'

'Yo, it's Jin. Got a new number. Who's Zack? That chick you got pregnant?'

'Shut up. And how did you know about that?'

'Bro, Mick told me. That gig at the Exford. I heard you bombed,' he said.

'Everyone bombed that night! There were only four people. Anyway, that doesn't matter. I'm not sure if I'm the dad.'

'Be careful, dude. She might be a gold digger.'

'She's definitely not a gold digger.'

'How do you know?'

'Because this mine is empty.'

'She doesn't know that,' Jin said. 'Man, you've been on TV. People think that means you're rich.'

'Once. I've been on TV once. She's not a gold digger,' I said again, but figured I could send her a screenshot of my bank balance just to be sure.

'Is she going to keep it?' Jin asked.

'Dude, I don't know what's going on. But if it's not my kid then it's none of my business.'

'True, true.' Jin paused. 'Good sex though?'

'I got to go, man. I'm expecting a call.'

'Alright, bro. You'll be sweet. I doubt your jizz even works.'

'Bye.' I threw the phone on the desk and flopped onto the chair, sinking down through the floor into the earth and down into hell. It felt like normal life.

7

THE MORNING AFTER ULTRASOUND DAY I still had no answers and no sitcom to watch.

I was in the kitchen warming up a bowl of frozen peas, wondering what would happen to my head if I stuck it in the microwave. Would it pop? It felt ready to explode anyway. It could fit in there but the door wouldn't close. Maybe there was a way to bypass the electronics so that it would turn on while the door was still open. I could find a thin bit of plastic or a wooden skewer to poke into the holes where the safety mechanisms were. Then it could still turn on. But would it get hot enough to pop my head? It would melt my eyeballs before it could give me that sweet combustion into carefree non-existence. Through the glass door, a pea exploded and I envied it. Maybe this whole idea was more about my feelings than the pursuit of science.

It's generous to describe what I was in as a kitchen. It was a sink in my lounge room. I had enough space in the living area for a fridge and a shabby old couch, both residing on a crummy grey carpet. My TV had been Dad's before he upgraded to a flatter one that he found during hard rubbish collection. The television lived on a dusty bookshelf that homed more DVDs than books. Most of the books I did have were either gifts from relatives who didn't know what interested me or novels I intended to read but never got around to.

An ad came on the TV for Tourism Western Australia. Great. It showed cute couples in fancy straw hats walking around artisan brew houses, people snorkelling in pristine blue water and women with shopping bags acting like they didn't have credit card debt. For a state that contained Perth, they had no mention of surprise pregnancies from one-night stands. There should have at least been a travel warning.

The second time that city nearly killed me was after a show. The crowd had been fun, drunk and playful, so I was on my way to 7-Eleven for a celebratory Cornetto. In the street, a man approached me looking a bit scruffy, or rather, a bit 'methy'. He wore grey tracksuit pants covered in food stains and had holes in his shirt. He almost had a tooth.

'I'm going to kill you!' he screamed.

'Wait, what?' I replied, stepping back.

'Yeah, I'm going to push you into traffic.' He curled his fingers at me, his pointy knuckles going hot white.

'Calm down, mate. It's all good,' I said, my palms open towards him.

'It's not all good!' he yelled. 'Get that fucking beard off your face!'

This was a hell of a demand, as *he* had a beard too. I wasn't privy to Perth's one-beard policy. How unlucky to have been caught with a beard by such a stringent local authority. The methy beard-law-enforcer tried to push me onto the road. I twisted in time to get out of the way. He withdrew a syringe from his tracksuit pants and jabbed it in my direction with a ferocious glare.

'I'll fuck'n stab ya,' he said, his eyeballs about to bulge out of his face and roll down the road.

'Alright, I'll shave my beard. I'll go do it now,' I said.

'Yeah, you better.'

'I will, I will.' I backed towards the road, my hands still raised. When I saw there were no cars coming, I bolted across and continued in whatever direction seemed less… druggy. It wasn't a big syringe but I was lucky I didn't end up with a punctured lung.

I checked on the peas. The top ones were still a bit frozen. I shut the microwave door again and it hummed back on. The memory of the third time I was almost killed in Perth began to drift over me, but my phone rang. Unknown number.

'Hello, this is Ben.'

'G'day mate, Zack Robinson here. I got your message.'

'Ah! Hey, mate!' I rushed over to the couch to find the remote. 'Thanks for ah…' It had fallen between the pillows. 'Thanks for the call'. I extracted the remote and tried to turn the TV off. The batteries were dead.

'Jesus, mate. Didn't expect to hear from you like this. How you feeling?' he said. I could barely hear him over the TV. I found the power cord and yanked it. I pulled too hard and the TV began to topple over. I shoved my shoulder against it just in time and leaned it back up.

'Yeah great. I mean not, ah, not great. It's all pretty confusing,' I said.

'I can imagine. Well look, I'm free around six tonight if you want to meet up and go through all the information you have. I can't promise I can give you any answers but I'll at least get you up to speed with how it all works.'

'That would be awesome of you, mate. Thank you.' The microwave had started beeping. I rushed over to it, almost tripping on a crease in the carpet. The microwave door opened to reveal that the peas had shrivelled. A cloud of vapour licked my face.

'No worries, would be good to catch up anyway. Someone said they saw you on TV doing comedy a while back? That's great to hear.'

'Oh yeah, thanks.' I kept forgetting I'd been on TV. It felt like I'd spent more time under one. This wasn't an apartment a television personality would live in. It was an apartment you'd see on a crime show where they found the murder suspect, hiding from the law and eating a bowl of shrivelled peas like a psycho.

'Where should I meet you?' I asked.

Zack told me to meet him near his office in St Kilda at a cafe called Lentil as Anything. It was on the other side of town. It would be a pain in the arse to get to and I really didn't feel like embarking on such a trek.

'Alright, I'll see you then,' I said.

I hung up, carried the bowl of peas into my room and slumped onto the floor to think everything over. I flicked at the peas to find any that weren't burnt to green raisins. I plucked out a few that were still round and threw them into my mouth before lying back to imagine my murky future.

The thoughts weighed my eyelids down until I fell asleep among the wasteland of my bedroom floor.

* * *

I woke up. It was 4:23 p.m. My bike was leaning against the wall opposite me. It would take me an hour and a half to ride to St Kilda. That would see me arriving around 6 p.m. I'd get some fresh air and much-needed exercise. It would be the best thing for me right now.

***

Fifty-six minutes later I was still curled up on the carpet. I messaged Zack to say I was on my way. This pressured me just enough to peel off the floor and call an Uber.

My bike looked dejected but I was late.

I left wearing the least unclean shirt I could find. The deodorant overpowered the smell of sweat that still hung in the armpits. Just.

I waited outside my apartment. It was an old building owned by a landlord who must have thought painting was a one-time thing. The faded, teal flakes peeled away just enough for spider webs to form and keep them attached to the miserable brick wall. I wanted to scamper back inside and dive onto the mattress but the car arrived. The driver was in his late forties. His hair was a bush of untamed curls and patches of grey. He appeared to be unaware that nose trimmers were a marketed product.

'Ben?' he checked.

'That's me.' I slouched on the back seat.

'How's your day been?' he said in a thick accent. Italian. Or Greek. He had a set of worry beads hung from the rear-view mirror. Maybe I could borrow them.

'Um.' I paused 'Good thanks.'

'You just finished work or off to work?'

'I don't work much,' I said, putting my seatbelt on.

'Really? What do you do?'

I swallowed a groan. He was one of the chatty ones.

'I'm a comedian so I usually work at night.' I glanced up at the mirror, catching the driver's mellow expression.

'Have to pay the bills, my friend. You have kids?' he asked.

'I don't know.' I went back to the window again. The driver laughed.

'Don't ever have kids. Very expensive,' he said.

'I'm sure you love them though, right?'

'Of course, I love my daughter. But so many bills. So many bills. School fees, uniform, books, gymnastics, Greek lessons…' he continued but I zoned out.

I wondered if I could drive for Uber. I'd have to buy a car first, so I'd need a loan. I hadn't done my tax return in a couple of years, so I'd have to sort that out to be able to apply. That would require an accountant but I couldn't afford one just yet. I'd have to make some money first. Maybe I could drive for Uber. Fuck.

The buildings of Melbourne's CBD ignored me as we drove by. They were filled with people with jobs and careers and money. Calls were being made about deals and deadlines. Printers were being jammed and fixed in minutes. Those buildings were giant machines and I was a cog that didn't fit; destined to roll along the ground collecting dust until I was covered in insignificance. I'd been a loose cog for too long now. The machines around me had updated and no longer had a place to put me. I couldn't think like a worker. I couldn't wake up in time for a meeting or feign interest in what Sandra in HR got up to on the weekend. Yes, I'm sure the winery was delightful, Sandra, no one cares.

The driver turning around in his seat snapped me out of my thoughts.

'Okay, my friend. We here,' he said.

'Thanks, mate. Have a good one.' I sprang from the car and scanned the apartment building in front of me. It stood about ten stories high with curved glass around the balconies, lit by warm orange lights. The outside stairs were lined by a dozen or so pot plants. The paint didn't have a single crack in it. I couldn't see the cafe anywhere. Google maps revealed that the driver had dropped me half a kilometre away. I was five minutes late already.

'Hey we're not quite…' I started back towards the Uber but he sped off. I bounded after him, sweat building on my back and underarms. He turned off and I couldn't see the car anymore. I kept up the run and found the street I needed. As I rounded the corner a tall figure hit me, almost knocking me out of the suburb.

'Oh shit, I'm so sorry I…'

'Ben?' He said squinting at me.

'Zack! Damn it, sorry. I thought I was late.'

Zack slapped my upper arm in reassurance. His blond hair hadn't been brushed in the ten years since I'd seen him last. It had thinned out some as well. He wore a corporate cream shirt under a tired black jacket. His physique still held its athletic form but with a thin layer of cushion added to it.

'Good to see you, mate.' He held out his hand. I didn't have time to wipe the sweat off my palm but he didn't flinch when he grabbed it.

I hid a wince. All his years of cricket had given Zack a gorilla grip.

'Thanks so much for doing this,' I said. 'I have no idea what's going on.' I'd finished with the handshake but he hadn't.

'You look like you haven't slept either.' He released my crumpled bones and continued in the direction he was facing. 'Lentil is this way.'

'I thought it was this way.' I pointed behind him.

'You're right, Tommo,' he said, evoking my schoolyard name. 'You really don't have any idea what's going on.'

Still a Snobinson.

'Lead the way.' I rubbed the joints in my fingers and followed the former cricket captain.

Lentil as Anything was a cosy cafe with red brick walls covered in mismatched art and a community notice board. It had a bohemian vibe and an aroma of spices I couldn't name. Zack and I sat down on cheap metal chairs at a small wooden table, right next to a man who appeared to be homeless. He wore three seasons worth of clothing, including a brown jacket and the smell of last year. Behind the metal counter, the staff spoke in fresh English, each with a different accent.

'I love how eclectic this place is,' Zack said.

'Yeah, it's ah… very St Kilda.'

'My office is just around the corner. Do you ever do shows in this area?'

'Sometimes,' I said. 'Last time I was out this way I was sitting in the park down the road there near the beach before a gig. I was under a palm tree, it was sunny. So nice. And right when I thought, "Why don't I come to St Kilda more often?" a junkie vomited onto my shoes.'

Zack laughed with a brief snort. It was more snort than laugh, though.

'That sense of danger just adds to the scenery,' he said, leaning back. 'It's so funny that you became a comedian.'

'That's a good start, then.'

It was crazy that he was a doctor but I didn't say so. Not that he wasn't smart enough. It just felt surreal that we were the same age and yet I didn't feel old enough to be a doctor. Zack Robinson somehow managed to live more years of life than me since we had finished school.

He waved over one of the staff with a flick of his eyebrows and ordered a coffee. I said I was fine with water.

'Okay, start from the top. What's the situation?' Zack's tone had dropped its geniality. It was now flat with a hint of that faux concern that medical professionals had trained to employ.

I took a deep breath and folded my arms. I peered over at the window only to catch a reflection of myself. My hair was sticking up at the back. I rubbed at it to get it under some control. Not that Zack could judge. He better not be judging. We can't all be doctors and play cricket and date women I have the hots for.

'I slept with a woman on April 29th,' I began. 'Then apparently she slept with another guy about a week later.' I got my notebook out of my back pocket and drew a timeline with all the dates on it. 'I don't know if it's exactly a week later, but it's a bit too sensitive to ask at the moment. So let's say a week.'

Zack peered down at my scribbles behind a stern expression. I wondered if he pushed-in lines at hospital cafeterias.

'The ultrasound says that she is seven weeks pregnant. I was confused because seven weeks ago was April 17th. That's over a week before I was with her. That was weird. Did she sleep with someone before me? So then I looked up a pregnancy calculator online to help me work out what was going on. And all these calculators kept asking for her last period.'

'Yes,' Zack said, 'pregnancies are dated from the last menstrual cycle.'

My eyes narrowed. Not at him, more at the medical industry in general.

'Why?'

'Well, mate, doctors don't know when a pregnant woman actually ovulated. Women mostly don't know either unless they are testing their cervical mucus. It could be day eleven of their cycle. It could be day seventeen. It could even be later than that. Also, it can be irregular. Most of the time women at least know when they started bleeding that cycle, so the pregnancy dating starts from that,' he said. But all I heard was 'VAGINA VAGINA VAGINA'.

'I think I understand.' I didn't.

'I'll put it this way,' he continued. 'You preheat a barbeque, *then* you put sausages on. The period is the preheating and the sausages are the sperm. So when do you start timing the whole process? From the preheating.'

'I don't really cook, but sure. You're saying you date the pregnancy from the start of the menstrual cycle, not from when the sperm hits the egg.'

'Yep. When a doctor says a woman is eight weeks pregnant, that's not how long ago conception happened,' he said.

'Ah okay, but this woman said she was on the pill and doesn't know when her period was.'

'Okay,' said Zack. 'If the date of the last period isn't known, the ultrasound adds the average day of ovulation.'

'What's the average day of ovulation?' I said. I was listening but also really wanted to slump off the chair and curl up into the foetal position again. I didn't, but only because the staff didn't deserve to deal with the mess.

'The universal average for ovulation is day fourteen, so it's two weeks,' he replied.

The pregnancy calculator was right. It had estimated the conception date based on subtracting the two weeks the ultrasound would have added. These two weeks were just the doctor's way of keeping the pregnancy date in the same format as women who knew their last period.

'So, like this?' I drew what I understood on the notepad.

Zack studied the graph. 'That's the one. Assuming the information is correct.' He shrugged.

'Assuming it is, is the kid mine?' I asked.

'Maybe.' His shambled hair flopped as he adjusted himself in his seat. 'Your sperm would have to last three days. That's possible if you have healthy sperm.'

'I do eat kale,' I said. Zack scoffed and shook his head. It was enough to settle my heart rate from 'critical' to 'bearable'. My shoulders relaxed into the discomfort of the metal chair.

'Maybe we can test to see if the baby is a smart-arse. Then we'll know for sure if it's yours.' His coffee arrived and he took a long sip to let me absorb everything. 'You're definitely in range,' he said after a while.

'Can the ultrasound just be wrong?' I asked.

'It can. The sonographer could have been shit,' he said. The doctor's tone had been replaced by one of the old schoolboy.

'Is that the medical term for it?' Too much sarcasm coloured my question. It came out ungrateful.

'It happens, mate.' He ignored my jibe. 'An ultrasound is only as good as the person conducting it. Plus these are all estimates. Even if the maths is correct, how do you know she's giving you the correct info?' he pressed.

'Come on, Zack. Why would she give me false info?'

'Let's put it this way,' he said. 'If a woman sleeps with two guys, gets pregnant and then gets this ultrasound dating, who does she think the father is?'

'The one closest to the conception date?' I said.

'The one she wants it to be.' He took another sip of coffee and placed his arms on the table like we were negotiating the terms of my surrender.

I released a heavy sigh. 'I get the sense that I'm not that guy.'

The smell from the homeless man intensified.

'I'm sorry, mate,' Zack said.

'Okay, but based on the best information we have, what are the odds? I pulled out, by the way.'

'The odds of withdrawal failure are between four and eighteen percent. Then the odds of sperm lasting a full five days are only around five percent but that's not based on reliable research. The odds of the ultrasound failure rate would be tricky to find…'

By the last statistic Zack's voice trailed off in my head. I was already having arguments with myself about whether to trust Tash. She told me that she slept with the other guy a week after me. I assumed that meant seven days. Maybe it was nine days, making him way off the ultrasound bullseye. Maybe it was five days. The internal chatter was interrupted by a sentence I didn't want to hear.

'So if the test is accurate, your odds are equally likely,' Zack said.

'Right, but how equally likely?'

Zack let out a long breath and paused. 'Doctors don't like to get into telling patients odds, mate. We come across enough exceptions to give us doubt.'

'I'm not a patient. I'm a guy who lent you a pen once, let's say it's returning the favour.'

'You did? That's a strange thing to remember.' His quizzical squint wanted a response but I didn't oblige. My resentment towards him over the years was beginning to feel petty.

'Look,' Zack continued, 'if the ultrasound is off by three days in your direction it is almost definitely you. If it's off by three days the other way, it's more likely the other guy. Your sperm wouldn't last more than seven days. You'd have to have bloody super sperm."

"Maybe I do."

"You don't. It's more likely that you get struck by lightning than your sperm lasting a week.'

My stomach bit into itself.

There was the third time I was almost killed in Perth. I was driving Jin's Kia Rio one afternoon when it started pouring down. Thunder cracked through the air and bounced around the apartment buildings. The sky was pissed off about something so I pulled over to find shelter. The windscreen of the car was just a blur and I didn't want to find out whether Jin had insurance by crashing into a nicer car. I found a spot, pulled over and opened the door, ready to bolt into the cover of an apartment lobby. In that moment, a streak of white light snapped down from the heavens and struck me. It felt like being punched in the back of the head. My body locked up and I fell out of the car onto the drenched pavement. My skin tingled from the zap but my insides felt like liquid magma. I remained grounded until my senses caught up to the speed of light. It took weeks to feel like myself again.

I skipped on recounting this story to Zack as I doubted he'd believe that's how I got super sperm.

'Is it mine or not?' I could hear my voice starting to waver. I hid my face with my palms. I didn't want the homeless guy to see me. Not like this.

'It's impossible to say for sure until a paternity test. There are a few options before the birth but you'd have to leave it with me to check on a few things. This isn't my field.' Zack crossed his arms.

The homeless guy made to leave. It was too much for him too.

'So I need to ask the mother for a paternity test. Until then, what do I do? Do I get involved with her or should I wait until I know for sure? I don't want to be a dick to her but also I don't want to get involved if it's not my place to.' I straightened my posture to sit like someone who knew how to be responsible. It was still crooked.

'That's not really a medical question, Tommo,' Zack said. 'I'll have to leave that one with you.'

Zack gave me a firm slap on the shoulder. I missed the homeless guy now. He'd been my real emotional support.

Before all the facts and figures had time to solidify in my head, Zack clapped his hands together and sat upright.

'Now you don't have to say yes, but while we're chatting, I was wondering if you could do me a favour?' he asked.

'Sure, of course.' I shrugged. 'I wouldn't have understood any of this without you. I mean, I barely do now but you've given me some clarity at least.'

'It's a gig,' he said.

'Great, I love gigs. I'll do it.'

'Hold on, hold on,' he said. 'It's not paid, I'm just desperate to find someone to do it at this point.'

'Mate, I'll do it.'

'You might hate me,' he warned. This was the least amount of hate I had ever felt towards Zack Robinson. He had helped. We never much associated with each other back in high school and that had created a misunderstanding on my behalf. He was kind and selfless outside of a tuckshop line. I couldn't see myself hating him beyond this point.

I returned the firm slap on the shoulder. 'That's a risk I'm willing to take.'

8

'I HATE YOU.'

I stood in front of Zack, adjusting the giant banana suit I was wearing.

'You look awesome, Tommo.' He was failing to suppress a grin.

We stood next to an outdoor stage, if you could use that word to describe four black wooden blocks shoved together. On it was a string quartet of high school students perched on plastic chairs, strangling their instruments into the crackling sound system. The concrete area of the playground of Ramsden Street Primary School was gated by a chain-link fence, decorated with balloons and a banner reading 'Tempting Fete'.

The tomato suit next to me was housing a pink-faced teenager, smiling his way through his simple existence. The sun reflected off his braces and burned my eyeballs out.

'I hope we get a crowd!' he screeched above his budding Adam's apple.

'Don't get too excited, champ,' I said. 'You don't want to get your sauce all over the stage.'

'What sauce?' He appeared concerned.

I rolled my eyes away and observed the table next to us. They were raffling off a giant meat tray: steaks, lamb chops and minced whatever it was. Despite it sitting under a plastic wrap in direct sunlight, this was the pinnacle of value for the attendees. One excitable, middle-aged couple were counting out every coin they had ever collected onto the table in exchange for tickets.

'Okay, so you know the drill. I'm going to field questions from the kids about eating healthy and you guys just be as silly as possible in response. Big smiles. Funny voices. I'll do all the real facts.' Zack was wearing a white lab coat and holding a clipboard.

'How come you're not fresh produce?' I asked.

'I'm a doctor, Ben.'

You could belittle anyone when you had a medical degree.

The quartet either gave up torturing their instruments or had killed them. Zack and only one other person clapped them as they collected their music stands and stepped off the fake stage. Zack hopped up and leant towards the mic. A screech from the speaker feedback made him jolt for a second before he addressed the hive of disinterested fete-goers.

'Hello Ramsden Street Primary! It's a beautiful day to be out and celebrating another year at the fete. I'm Doctor Zack and I'd like to invite some of my friends from the supermarket to talk to us about how healthy eating can be fun!'

The sound tech was one of Zack's kids, readied with an iPhone. She allowed an awkward silence to arrive before hitting play. A jovial tune squeaked out of the speakers. This was my cue to dance over to Zack but the bottom of the banana suit kept getting caught on the edge of the stage. It took me a few awkward tries to get up at all. The tomato and I waved our hands at a few traumatised toddlers gaping at us.

'Okay, who knows what this is?' Zack asked, pointing to me.

'I know! I know!' Yelled one kid, in a sports hat with a skateboard under his arm. He was too old to be proud of this knowledge.

'How about we let the younger kids have a guess?' Zack suggested in a tone befitting an amateur children's entertainer.

'It's a banana!' The kid said anyway. I would have accepted 'failed comedian' too.

'Nice work, mate! And what about this?' Zack did the same in reference to the teenage red boy.

A toddler in three-quarter pants and a Spiderman hoodie climbed onto the stage. Zack was too busy trying to inject enthusiasm into his search for an answer to notice. The kid's head was huge compared to his body. It seemed to weigh him forward as he walked. He trotted towards me with his arms outstretched. I wasn't prepared for a hug but I assumed wrong anyway. The kid punched me in the curve of my banana.

'Careful there, little mate,' I said, protecting my external organs.

It was too late. This young pioneer had started a toddler uprising. A bunch of other small humans, with animal face paint and cordial stained shirts, charged onto stage to join the impromptu game of assault the banana. I dodged and weaved to avoid the tiny fists of fury. Zack tried to usher some of the stubby beasts away. The stage wasn't designed for… well it wasn't designed at all, but in particular not for lots of erratic feet stomping around it. It began to separate at the gaps between the blocks. In the interests of health and safety, I hopped from one to the other, but the bottom of the banana got caught again and sent me sideways towards the raffle table. I missed one of the parents selling tickets by the skin of my suit and landed square on the meat tray, the table collapsing underneath me.

Zack made a concerned yelp. The kids were shrieking with joy. The tomato was being chased by the skateboarder. Zack came over to me as I rolled my way out of a pool of squashed sausages. He checked that I was okay before addressing the newfound crowd of people rubbernecking.

'Looks like it's mashed banana for afternoon tea!' he said.

That pained me more than the fall.

***

I cycled home smelling of raw lamb and thinking about fatherhood.

A lot of parents at the fete seemed to be there to absolve themselves of responsibility for their kids, rather than take it. It had been far too long before any of them stepped in to quell the mini riots. Perhaps parenthood was a game of seeing how far you could wander away from your offspring before you had to do damage control.

There was a buzz in my pocket. I hopped off my ride and leaned it against a pole. It slipped and crashed to the pavement. I left it where it fell. I'd given up on expecting anything to work out for me today.

'Tash?' I answered.

'Hey.' She sounded distant, like it was a burden to call.

'Hey. Ah, how you feeling?'

'I'm not vomiting as much anymore, so that's good,' she said.

'That will happen when you stop going to The Court.'

'I meant the morning sickness.'

'I know,' I replied

'Oh,' she said. 'I forget you're a comedian.'

'So do my audiences.'

Not even a chuckle.

'Well, um yeah,' she faltered. 'I'm in Melbourne and look I know I haven't been making this easy on you and I'm sorry. I'm not trying to be an arsehole, it's just a lot. You know?'

'Wait. You're here?' I turned behind me, half-expecting to see her standing in the street.

'Yeah, I was visiting my cousin for her engagement party. But I wasn't sure about meeting up, I mean, I feel like I owe it to you to at least talk it all over and I know we are a bit confused and you don't have to see me…'

'Hey, hey, hey. Yes, we can meet up. That's cool. That's fine,' I said.

'Okay cool. I just don't want us to argue the whole time,' she said. 'I can't handle another all-nighter.'

'No, we don't have to argue. We don't have to even talk about that stuff if you don't want to.'

'What are we going to do then?' she asked.

'Um.' I bit my bottom lip. 'Are you free tonight?'

9

'THAT WAS GREAT,' Tash said, smiling. I had forgotten she did that.

I collected the sweat on my brow with the back of my wrist. My heartbeat was returning to normal. My face felt flush, which made me embarrassed, which made me blush.

'Yeah, it was fun,' I said, pouring myself a glass of water. 'Thanks for coming.'

'No worries,' she said, with an impish smirk. 'I'm glad I did.'

'Hey, that was great.' Another woman said as she walked past.

'Thanks for coming,' I said.

'Yeah, you were really funny.' An older man in a charcoal suit walked by with his much younger wife.

'I appreciate that, thank you.' I turned back to Tash. 'Want to hang around for a bit?'

'I don't want to prevent you from seeing all your fans,' she said nodding her head towards the audience leaving The Comic's Lounge showroom. It was as large as a ballroom, filled with long tables and black drapes hanging from the roof. The carpet could have been lifted from a casino; the once intense colours long faded under tipsy patrons' feet. Decades of splashed beer and spirits created sticky patches that pulled at the soles of your shoes. Twenty years ago it had been a strip club. That's why it felt so wholesome now.

'Ha! They're not really *my* fans. They were here to see whoever was on.' I shrugged and sprang onto the barstool with zero grace.

'They are now.' Tash raised her eyebrows at something behind me. I swivelled to see a young couple approach. The guy was wearing a basketball cap and a blue hoodie. He glanced between me and Tash.

'Sorry to butt in. Just wanted t'know if we could grab a photo?' he said.

'Yeah of course.' I hopped back off the barstool. The young woman with him put her arm around me and faced the camera, adjusting her bleached white hair. We smiled longer than was comfortable.

'Do you want to get in?' Tash offered to the blue hoodie. 'I can take it for you.'

'Nah,' he said, too fast in my opinion. His phone's fake shutter sound went off three times in quick succession. He clicked another button and squinted at the screen. 'Cheers, bro.'

The couple left down the club's stairs with the rest of the crowd, most of which, I noticed, hadn't asked for a photo with me. Tash and I both took stools. I rested an elbow on the bar but I was sitting too far back for it to look natural. Instead, I leaned my weight back but there wasn't enough support on the stool. I found the most awkward position manageable and committed to it.

Only a few audience members remained in the bar area now. The bucks parties and hens nights had filed out into the wilderness. They'd been pretty rowdy during the show but in an audience that size you could ignore the ruckus from the stage. Addressing a large group of drunk people to get a bonus laugh was often not worth the risk. If Tash hadn't been there, I might have attempted it out of negligence.

'Where do you get your material from?' Tash asked.

'From crazy things that happen to me, mainly,' I said.

'Are you going to do jokes about the pregnancy?'

'Um.' I looked around the bar to see if there were any emergency exits. 'I don't know really. Hey, do you want a drink?'

'Sure,' Tash said, accepting the change of subject.

'I don't even know what you do, by the way,' I said, hoping to keep the conversation moving further away from questions about me.

'That's pretty weird,' she said. 'I guess we haven't spoken about that sort of stuff. I'm studying fashion at uni and I work in a bar.'

'Fashion is cool. How's my outfit?' I pulled at the collar of my white, spotted shirt. It had a yellow stain on the bottom part but I hid that by never keeping the rest of it too clean. My jeans were skinny and black like everyone else my age in this city.

'You could use some work,' she said, then poked her tongue out at me.

'Ouch.' I grinned. I waved the barman over. Tash reached into her bag, pulling out her purse.

'I've got this,' I said, gesturing an open hand over her bag like I was using Jedi powers to close it. 'Comics drink for free.'

'I guess that means I'm a comic now?' She put her purse away. 'I think I'm pretty funny, at least.'

'Oh yeah? Got a joke for me?'

'Yep, ready? What did Sushi A say to Sushi B?'

'What?' I asked, though I knew this one.

'Wassa-B!?' She laughed throughout the punchline, which made me laugh. 'It's pretty good, I think,' she said. 'Hey, I wanted to ask: did you actually used to be a tradie like you said on stage?'

'Totally true. I was a carpenter for a couple of days when I was seventeen. I still feel sore from the day's work.'

'Tradies are overrated anyway,' she said, adjusting her bracelets.

'I know, right? They don't even know basic joke structure.'

She smiled and touched my shoulder with a light brush of her hand. My adrenaline bubbled back up. It urged me to pull Tash aside and ask her what the fuck we were going to do about the child. The lingering audience members kept me from breaking the light-hearted facade.

The bartender, Baz, came over wearing a grin I never saw when I was by myself. He had worked here for longer than I could write a joke. He was around when I did my first ever gig here. I died a horrible death. An absolute total of no laughs. My beardless face must have been so bereaved afterwards that Baz approached me and rested a hand on my shoulder.

'Even the best eat shit sometimes,' he had said. You could hear such poetry from a working-class man.

'What can I get'cha?' he said to Tash.

'I'll have a Furphy please,' I said, instead.

'I'll just have a soda water,' said Tash.

'You're not drinking?' asked Baz.

'No I can't because, I… um.' Tash turned to me, going red.

'I am!' Libby fluttered in between us. 'I'll get a Furphy too.'

'Too easy.' Baz spun around to get two bottles out of the fridge behind him, placed them on the bar and popped them open for us. He poured a soda water for Tash, then busied himself with people down the other end of the bar. We all waited for him to do this before Libby cut through the stiff air around us.

'I'm Libby.' She clinked her bottle to Tash's glass.

'Natasha. I loved your set.'

'Not mine?' I teased to no response.

'Thank you so much!' Libby cocked her head. 'Do you watch much comedy?'

'Yeah, online mostly but some big names come to Perth every now and again.'

'Oh you're from Perth, that's cool.' Libby managed to sneak a glance at me. 'Who are your favourite comedians?'

'You, obviously.' Tash grinned.

'Obviously.' Libby waved a hand over her hair and chuckled. I was just waiting to be included again.

'Um, I like Wil Anderson,' Tash said. 'And I saw Amy Schumer when she was out here. Her comedy's pretty dirty but I love her. And do you like Kitty Flanagan?'

Libby was distracted. She was tugging at my shirt away from Tash's view, but I didn't know how to respond without being seen. If she wanted to say something she could wait.

'What was that, sorry?' Libby checked.

'Do you like Kitty Flanagan?' Tash repeated.

'Yes! I've done a gig with her actually.'

'No way! That must have been so good,' said Tash.

'She's the nicest,' said Libby 'And her comedy is so smart. She recently did this amazing routine about coffee wankers and I was laughing so hard but also crying because I'm totally one of them.'

'God, I better not watch it then. I am too. I just think almond milk needs to be more of a thing.'

'Totally,' Libby said, nodding. 'And hey if you like Amy Schumer then watch Ali Wong. She is so much better. Not to diss Amy, but Ali Wong's last special was freaking amazing. She comes out on stage and she is clearly…'

Libby hesitated. That special she was referring to *was* amazing and Tash *would* love it, but Ali Wong was seven months pregnant in it. I'm glad Libby realised this because I didn't want Tash to know that Libby knew about our maybe baby.

Libby turned to me, caught the look I was sending her way and coughed out an excuse to leave her sentence unfinished. 'Actually, Ben, I better ask before I forget. Have you got a second to help me with something backstage?'

'Sure,' I replied. Turns out Libby couldn't wait. I looked to Tash. 'You good out here for a minute?'

'Yeah, all good,' she replied. She chuckled at a thought and then called after me. 'I'm going to talk to the owners about doing a comedy skit with all my bad jokes.'

'Sweet.' I made the okay sign with my fingers. 'But I'm pretty sure

I've cornered that market. I'll be back in a sec.'

Libby and I pushed our way through the aisles between empty seats. I parted the curtain and walked behind the stage to the green room.

'What's up?' I asked.

Libby clicked the door closed behind her. I flopped onto the red lips sofa, bumping my head on the counter above it. My clenched teeth had to stop four-letter words from flying out.

'That's her, right?' she said.

'Yeah, that's her.' I picked up an empty water bottle from the coffee table and picked at the label.

'Poor girl. I'm glad she's not alone. Does she know that I know?'

'Nope.'

'Okay, I won't say anything.' Libby took a swig from her beer.

'I think it's nice that we're just trying to be normal. Whatever that is.' I peeled the label off the bottle and wrapped it around my fingers.

'I'm proud of you, she needs some support. But also, you know, what if it's not yours? Will you still raise the kid with her?'

'Fuck, Libby I don't know. I can't even work out what I'm doing today let alone if that happens.'

'Well just don't lead her on, okay?' Libby said.

'Lead her on!?'

Libby's eyes went large above her thin, pursed lips.

'Come on,' I said.

'Just, be careful.'

'Whatever, mate. I don't know what to do. I'm either a good dude for being there for her or an arsehole for leading her on. What am I supposed to do? She contacted me!'

'Hey, don't get upset. I'm just—'

'You're just what? Helping? Because it feels worse now.'

'Fine.' She tilted her wrist up for another swig.

I dug my heels into the couch to lever myself up, passed Libby without looking at her and swung the door open.

'What would you do in my situation?' I asked, still holding onto the handle. Libby shrugged.

'Shit myself,' she said.

'I'm way past that.'

***

Back at the bar, Tash was chatting to Baz, giggling at something he'd just said. That was meant to be my job. This is what happens when you put your career on pause to be berated by a friend, the bar staff take over. Baz clocked me.

'Here he is,' he said.

'Here I am.'

'Here you are,' Tash said, flashing her eyebrows. 'You going to finish your beer?'

The bottle of Furphy stood on the bar, ready to forgive me for leaving it. The stool next to Tash called me over too.

'Um,' I said, squinting up at the ceiling so my eyeballs didn't fall out from the swell of feelings under them. 'I might just head off.'

'Oh, okay,' Tash got off her stool and pulled her bag strap over her shoulder. 'It was nice to meet you, Baz.'

'You too. Come back any time.' He winked and then gave me a thumbs up. I joined Tash.

'Hey, sorry. I just think I better head home,' I said.

'It's okay, I can drive you. I have my cousin's car.'

'No, no. It's just down the road. I'm all good. I'll walk you to your car though.'

'Okay,' she said. It was strange how even such a short word could carry disappointment.

We took the stairs down to the street. The wind picked up and pushed us around as we found her cousin's Prius. Tash turned back to me, her arms folded as she began to shiver.

'It's cold now. Let me drive you,' she said.

'No seriously, it's all good.'

I stopped walking, so she did as well. Then I hugged her without meaning to. Our cheeks brushed against each other but they were too cold from the wind to feel anything. She gave me a slow pat on the back but didn't put her arms around me. I pulled away when I couldn't handle the lack of reciprocity.

'Sorry,' I said. 'I just feel overwhelmed by the idea of a kid and I don't know if you even want me to be around and…'

She saw the regret on my face and hugged me back. The warmth from our bodies met and held us in place. The wind became louder and colder but it could no longer get our attention. We let the moment fade away at its own pace, so we didn't have to speak. Her shivers returned and I rubbed her arms.

'I don't want you to think I'm hitting on you, that's all,' she said with a soft curl of her lips.

'Don't worry,' I said. 'I would never get involved with someone who drives a Prius.'

Tash laughed and pushed me backwards.

'Always a comedian,' she said. 'I'm glad we met up. Thanks for not running away when I said I was pregnant. It's a relief to know you'll step up if it's yours.'

I dropped my head and nodded. The relief hadn't found me yet.

'I should let you go,' Tash said.

'Okay, I'll let you let me go.'

My phone vibrated. Tash got into the car and drove off with the silence only an awkward moment and a hybrid vehicle could hold. Libby was calling.

I pressed decline.

10

EVERYTHING WAS TASH. The morning sunlight coming through my crooked blinds was her warmth. The sound of the breeze was her calming voice. The pillow I was holding was her body. It was also her face. It was also her boobs. I'd just been hugging a pillow for an hour. When I had woken up I pulled it close to me to cope with the thumping in my chest. It also gave me something to do with my arms instead of reaching for my phone and messaging her. I drafted a few texts in my head that I'd never let reach my fingers. They were all variations of: 'Hey just wanted to say thanks for seeing me yesterday and come hold me forever.' Each time I considered what I should do with my day my mind flicked back to Tash. *It's not mine. Maybe. Not sure.* Tash's eyes were in front of mine, then I'd blink and Libby was scolding me for being so close.

I shook my head to bring my mind back into the room. It was just as messy. Between the clothes, empty bowls and tissues, there was a bit of scrap paper crumpled up on the carpet. I reached for it, crawling across the bed without getting out, and unfolded it. It was my set list from the night before. It included my classic crowd-pleasers from 'gay or vegetarian' to 'my balls are weird'. Before I went on stage I had scribbled it down on Libby's notepad and tore the page off. Those jokes hadn't been delivered to a crowd for a year. It was my reliable material that I had only trotted out so that Tash didn't hear my new stuff. The paper crumpled in my frustrated fist and I threw it at the wall in place of throwing myself. It bounced off and landed in about the same spot as I'd picked it up from.

Melbourne's chill crept in through the gap in my window. There were no notifications on my phone. Facebook confirmed there were no notifications. Twitter did the same. It had been weeks since my last Tweet and I was missing the dopamine from the likes.

@BenThomasComedy:

Every time you take a photo of your food, remember that there are kids in Africa that don't even have Instagram.

Six likes. Three retweets. That deserved more. I retweeted it myself: a trick to get the joke more exposure without having to write a new one. I checked Facebook, Snapchat, Tumblr and then went back to Twitter to see no new action. The phone went down. Then back up. I opened the Twitter app once more as if my eyes were expecting to see something different. It startled me when they did. The incoming call screen had popped up.

'Tash?' I answered.

'Hey, Ben.'

'Um. Hey!' I rose from the bed as if I needed to greet her standing up.

'How are you?' she asked.

'I'm good. How are you?' I paced in circles.

'Good.' She didn't need to say any more. She sounded warm and sweet in just one syllable.

'What's up?' I asked.

'Listen, I leave tomorrow afternoon so I thought maybe we could catch up one more time before I leave. It would be good to just go over the situation, especially now that we're not bickering anymore.'

'Yeah!' I answered way too loud to give off any casual vibe. *Come on, Ben. Keep it chill.* 'Um, yeah let's meet up this afternoon?'

'Sure, I'm free after five. I can come to you if you like,' she said.

Since I had first learned of the pregnancy, the mess in my place had built up as if it were a personal project. The couch pillows were on the floor. The kitchen benchtop was crammed with dirty plates and cups. The blinds had been pulled up with only one of the multiple strings so that the slats sat askew across the window. The view from my lounge was of the rooftops facing north, covered in spots of moss, leading away from the city, becoming cheaper as they ran into the outer suburbs. Even they were untidy.

'Yeah.' I meant to say no. Neutral territory would be far more sanitary. 'Actually, how about we meet at a bar though,' I said.

'I can't drink, remember?'

'Yeah, of course. Ah. Maybe come around here?' I bit my tongue. Hard. I was better without it anyway. The apartment was even more disgusting on a second look. Maybe I could burn it all down and build a clean, new one.

'Sure. Text me your address,' she said, without seeming to know that her acceptance would jolt me. We hung up, not before more awkward stuttering from me, aided by my now sore tongue.

I became a blur, sweeping through the rubble of my lifestyle. In the first five minutes, the mess went from outright chaos into segregated piles of disaster. I changed tack and showered. It gave me time to panic in the comfort of warmth. Then I dried and accepted my clothing options were either creased but clean or smooth but smelly. The final selection was a fresh, wrinkled t-shirt and a pair of jeans that I spun around like a helicopter propeller to get some of the old sweat smell out. The jeans were black with a curry stain on the pocket so I found a Sharpie and coloured it in to hide it.

Racing down to the local grocery store, I bought surface sprays and cloths, both of which I'd always deemed luxury items. I also asked the owners for something to help improve the air quality of my place. The old couple didn't stock scented soy candles but they assured me that the plug-in air freshener was delightful.

When I finished doing the dishes, straightening the blinds, and vacuuming up morsels of food that I didn't even remember having, the place still didn't look decent. It just looked decent enough to maybe get my bond back one day. It was as if a responsible person had made a solid attempt to clean up after a committed derelict. The carpet still exposed years of neglect but at least there weren't any burned peas still hanging around… that I could see.

A knock at the door made me drop the surface spray. I snatched it back up, threw it into a cupboard and answered. I checked my breath. It needed some surface spray but it was too late.

'Hey.' Tash stood in front of me, a pink tote bag over her shoulder with a print of a barking dog above the name 'Keith Haring'. I wondered if that was an ex-boyfriend of hers. A black dress hung over her body under a navy cardigan. The dress was loose enough to cover any signs of a second visitor. I think she was wearing make-up, but in the style that women sometimes do to make it appear like they're not wearing much make-up.

'Hey,' I replied. She didn't attempt to hug me so I gestured her through. 'Come in. The place is the cleanest it's ever been so if it's not up to your standards I can't help you.'

'It looks clean to me,' she said.

I watched her take in the apartment to see if there were any signs of her lying. She smiled, which made me do so too. She clung to her tote bag, observing all the not-much my apartment had to showcase.

'Have you eaten?' I asked.

'Not really.'

'I know this great recipe if you like. It's called ordering Thai food.'

'Sure.' She shrugged.

We sat on the couch to go through the menu. Tash might have smelled nice but I couldn't tell because the apartment was filled with the scent of 'Garden Escape'. After we'd ordered she took off her shoes and crossed her legs on the couch. I curled a bare foot under my bum and forced myself to recline. She was here. On my couch. About to share a meal with me that I hope she would split the bill for.

I sucked at my tongue to stop questions about the paternity test from leaving my mouth. If one escaped it would be followed by dozens of others about what date she slept with the other guy, who she thinks the dad is, and whether we should just get married right now to prevent people from judging us. The Comic's Lounge would be great for the reception.

Instead, I glared out the window as if there was something of interest there. She could raise the subject if she was confident we could stay cool about it. Tash got up and went to my bookshelf.

'I'm going to judge your books,' she said.

'I haven't read any of those. They are just what I want people to think I've read. I've got picture books in my cupboard.'

'You're a dork.' She tilted a book of selected short stories towards herself. 'Did you write these?'

'Me?' I asked, confused.

'Yeah, because they're *short* stories.' She raised her eyebrows to sell the line but abandoned it before I had a chance to chuckle. 'Sorry. Lame joke.'

I gave her the chuckle all the same. 'That's how I'd know if your body was ever taken over by aliens. Lame jokes prove it's the real you.'

'Maybe aliens got to me yesterday, you wouldn't know.' She cocked her head.

'The night we met you made a "ladies first" joke when we got into the cab,' I told her.

'You remember that?' she said.

'You don't?'

Tash turned back to the bookshelf. 'Hey look, you have Scrabble!'

'Are you using a boardgame to change the subject?' I smiled.

'Like you used getting us drinks to change the subject last night?' Her eyebrows were back up.

'Ah yes! Scrabble. Let's play,' I said, accepting defeat.

'Are you any good at it?' she asked.

'I'm awesome if misspelling is allowed.'

She grinned and shrugged. 'It could be fun.' She handed me the box, which was covered in dust. The day's cleaning hadn't extended to the forgotten realm of my bookshelf.

We set up on the coffee table. We got comfortable on the floor and collected up the requisite tiles. I gasped at one of my tiles and put it back in the pile.

'You can't do that!' she snapped.

'Sorry, I'm allergic to bad letters. I should have mentioned that.' I took it back grinning.

'You're weird.' She furrowed her brow.

'Thanks for noticing.' I ran my fingers through my fringe. 'My sister always beat me at this game.'

'I was going to ask if you have siblings. Older or younger?'

'Older. Do you have any?'

'Only child,' she said.

'That explains a lot.' I put as much sarcasm into my voice as possible. It was a blunder to assume people who didn't know you too well would realise you're only teasing. There had been countless times I'd mocked someone at a party without them knowing my sense of humour. They'd try to hide a grimace and say they had to go to the bathroom or catch a helicopter, then they wouldn't return. Delivery is everything.

'Yeah, I'm so awesome my parents didn't need to keep trying.' She gave me back the same tone.

'Good one.' She was learning my ways. 'Oh hey, how was the engagement party?'

'Tedious,' she said. 'The dresses were glorious though.'

'Hey, save those big words for the Scrabble board. If those letters aren't missing.'

She chuckled. Just a fraction.

Making Tash laugh became my game for the night. It was easier than trying to win at Scrabble and saved me from checking for Twitter notifications I knew wouldn't come. She asserted she could play words like 'QI' and 'ZA' because they were accepted in Words with Friends. Those got her hefty scores. I knew 'LMAO' wasn't a word but it was worth hearing her object with language inconsistent with pending maternity.

The food arrived, which we both only picked at. I ate a few pieces of the tofu from around the noodles of my pad thai because my stomach was slow to digest my nerves. Lo-fi hip-hop beats played on my laptop to keep the sound of our chewing from becoming the soundtrack of the night. Tash shuffled over to it after giving up on a spring roll. She asked me if she could pick a song. She'd already paused the music and opened YouTube. I said sure, to play along with the non-question. Tash found a video of 'You Only Live Once' by The Strokes. It sounded like a demo version of the song, recorded on a home microphone and a keyboard, making it feel raw and intimate. An interesting choice for someone who wasn't hitting on me.

'My dad used to be in a band,' she said. 'I think Mum was a groupie but they have never admitted it. They just said they met at a gig at one time. Anyway, Dad says that when my cousin gets married he wants to get the band back together for the reception. I'm kind of like, oh god no, but also I kind of want to experience it.'

All my brain gave me to say was *Yeah, like smelling your own farts!* so I stayed quiet. My strategy to get Tash to like me was to avoid being me. She picked up a tile from the Scrabble board and turned it over in her fingers.

'I love Melbourne.' She went on. 'I was thinking of moving here after uni. Way more opportunities for fashion design.'

'Yeah?'

'Yeah. I follow this girl on Instagram that makes her own jewellery and she just got picked up by a French label because they saw her stuff at Melbourne Fashion Week.'

'That's crazy,' I said, bored at my own offering. There wasn't much more I could contribute other than childish jokes or my desperate questions about the other potential father. The Strokes had created the wrong mood for either of those.

'So crazy,' Tash said. 'I want to make my own jewellery line one day.'

'I bet you could,' I said.

'Maybe.'

'Maybe? I tell dick jokes for money. If I can live my dream…'

She laughed. A proper laugh that cut through the music.

'True.' She smiled.

I rose to put the leftovers in the fridge. When I turned back, Tash was lying down on the couch caressing a cushion. I retrieved a pillow from my room and brought it back to lie on the floor.

'I'm sorry.' She whispered so low I almost missed it.

'What for?' I asked.

She didn't reply for a few breaths.

'I'm sorry that I'm putting so much pressure on you.'

Questions I'd been holding back surfaced before I could stop them.

'Where's the other guy, can I ask?'

'Perth,' she said.

'How did he take the news?'

'He's an arsehole.'

That was enough to give me pause, but there was an image forming in my mind that needed a few more colours.

'What, um,' I continued, 'what does he do?'

'He's a football player.'

'Like AFL?'

'No, just a state team,' she said. 'But reckons he can't look after a kid while he's hoping to get into the national league.'

'I'm sorry. I think I said the same sort of thing when you first told me.'

'It's okay. I get it. No one wants me to have this kid.'

I squirmed a bit. 'Well, it just doesn't seem like, you know, it doesn't seem like the best situation is all.'

'I have to keep it,' Tash said. Before I could respond, she continued. 'I never told you but I lost a kid.'

The music might have still been playing but I didn't hear it now. Tash's restrained voice made the apartment feel small. The walls were creeping in on us.

'I got pregnant when I was eighteen,' she said. 'It was with my boyfriend at the time and he was super supportive. But I had a miscarriage and that fucked me up.'

'Tash, I'm sorry,' I said.

'And we broke up because I couldn't handle being with him after that.'

We both just continued to stare at the ceiling. It was amazing how not looking at each other could open people up. It was why old-school dads took their sons out fishing instead of having a coffee. They could absorb the ocean view and express what few truths they wanted to share without the dreaded emotional intensity of eye contact. When I was around ten, Dad decided it was time to tell me about the 'birds and the bees'. He rented a VHS of *Jurassic Park* for us while Penny was out at her friend's place. Watching the dinosaur thriller as he spoke was Dad's way of diffusing the awkward task of describing which human parts made more humans.

'I lost my mum,' I said.

The ceiling was grey in the dim light. My dad's years of sadness projected above me. They melted down and formed a puddle on the floor where I lay. He did so much for me during those years. If it wasn't *Jurassic Park* it was *Indiana Jones* or *Star Wars*. They helped me escape. Helped *us* escape. Entertainment was sometimes just distraction.

'Ben I'm—'

'It's okay, it was a long time ago. I don't even remember her.' The tone of my voice was grey too. 'There were some complications during my birth that she never recovered from. I never thought it was my fault but I always worried that my dad or sister felt that way.'

Tash's touch found its way to my shoulder. Her gaze discovered mine.

'It's not your fault,' she said. Our hands met in a brief squeeze.

'I know.' I nodded. 'Tash, listen. I don't know about the footballer guy but if I'm the dad I'll be there.'

The talking ended at that. Tash's eyes soon closed and her breath went soft. The laptop beeped to say its battery was low. I just closed it and returned to the floor. I lay awake in the darkness, which was softened by a distant glow of a street lamp, trying to stop imagining a future I didn't have yet. Tash's presence added to the gentle atmosphere the Garden Escape had created. Having a panic attack right now would just be lousy hospitality.

At 6 a.m. I got up, only having blinked a dozen times since lying down, and settled in my bedroom to watch the sun bring colour to my walls until sleep had its way.

11

A CALL FROM LIBBY woke me at around 1 p.m.

'Yo,' I croaked at her, getting up to see that Tash had gone.

'Still mad at me?' Libby asked.

I sighed. 'Yes.' I smirked at my own sarcasm.

'Good.'

'I wasn't really mad at you,' I said, 'just annoyed at the whole… you know.'

'I do know. What are you up to?' She spoke faster than usual.

'Not much. Just casually going out of my mind.'

'That's better than formally going out of your mind,' she said.

'I'd have to buy a suit to do that.'

'Maybe just rent one.' She had to have the last quip. 'Hey, so I'm in your area. You home?'

'Kind of.' I yawned.

'What do you mind kind of?' she asked.

'Yes, I'm around. Just waking up.'

'Great, I'll see you soon.' She stayed on the call to see how much of a fight I'd put up.

'Okay.' I waved a white flag. 'Do I have time to shower?'

'I'm like five minutes away, so maybe.'

I jumped in the shower. Too fast. I slipped on the tiles and caught the tap handle just in time to stabilise myself. It snapped off. Shoving it back in place didn't take. Libby messaged to say she was downstairs. I wrapped a towel around myself, went out to the kitchen area and clattered around in the drawers. There was a garlic press that had been left behind by the last tenants, which I'd never used. In the bathroom, I clamped it onto the metal rod that remained where the handle had been and turned it just enough to shut the water off. I put the same clothes back on and fled out the door.

As I approached Libby's Mitsubishi Mirage I waved with both arms to make her laugh. A peace offering, if anything.

'Get in loser, we're getting coffee,' she said through the crack of the window.

'You're buying.' The door clicked open with a careful tug. I'd broken enough things today. 'I spent all my money pretending I could afford dinner.'

The inside of the car looked like it had just been cleaned but I knew that Libby had never let it get dirty. There was nothing unneeded inside excepted for a plastic pomegranate charm hanging from the rear-view mirror. It smelled as if she'd emptied a whole can of Garden Escape into it. Resting on the shiny steering wheel, her hands were shaking.

'You nervous, mate?' I pointed at them. She rubbed them together like she was washing her hands.

'It's been a day. I've had four coffees already,' she said.

'Four!? What happened?'

'Dane got made redundant so I was running around trying to sort things out with the bank and our accountant.'

'Shit, that sucks. When did that happen?' I asked.

'About a week ago.'

'I didn't know that.'

'You've been preoccupied.' She didn't mean it to sting me but it did. My friendships had been pretty one-directional for a few weeks now.

'I want to talk to you about something important.' Her tone shifted. 'Let's find a cafe.' Her Mirage zipped onto the road and we heard a beep from an SUV behind her. 'Shit, I didn't even see him.'

Her hands were shaking even more.

'Take it easy, mate. Let's head to Fitzroy,' I said.

'Okay. And why did you have to pretend to afford dinner?'

'It's not important.'

'Who were you with?' she pressed.

The houses flicked by the window but it was still possible to jump out at this speed.

'Tash,' I admitted.

'Really!?' She stretched out the word so it would embarrass me for as long as possible. She might have been grinning but I refused to check.

The car ride felt like a drivers licence test. Libby was still jittery and I was too busy worrying about the road to make conversation. My legs pushed out to hold me in place as she made sharp turns. Maybe it was punishment for neglecting to check on her life's problems.

Libby found a park near a cafe called Queen of Spades, which only took her fourteen attempts to back into. She swore in another language, which was equal parts aggressive and adorable. We went in. The walls were rustic handmade brick in a dozen shades of brown. The brightest colours in the place came from the boardgame boxes that stood upright on every surface. Libby found a table furthest from the window with the most privacy. People we passed on the way were smiling and chatting over cardboard mats and plastic miniatures.

'Is there a game you want to play?' I asked.

'See if they have Flux,' she said. 'That's my favourite.'

There was a deck of Flux on the shelf near us. It was a black box with bright coloured letters on it and a picture of a moon. The playtime said five-to-thirty minutes. Even ultrasounds had better estimates.

'How do you play this?' I said, pulling the cards from the box and turning them over in my hand.

'You draw a card and then play a card until someone wins.'

'How do you win?' I frowned.

'That depends on the cards you draw and play.' Libby picked up the box and read the rules out to me. I didn't understand any better when she finished. She was delaying the mystery conversation, which I both didn't want and couldn't wait to be over.

'Wait, so the rules change depending on what cards we play?' I asked.

'Yes, you'll pick it up. Just play a rule card or an objective card until one of us wins.'

'I suppose I'll just guess my way through it then.'

'You do that a lot,' she said. Libby picked at the nail on her thumb and then began to chew it.

I put the cards down.

'Right, what's the important chat you want to have?' I asked. My eyebrows furrowed but I made no attempt to soften them.

Libby's eyes twitched.

'Okay, so don't get mad but I did some research for you,' she said.

'What research?'

'You can get a paternity test before the kid's born.'

'I can!?' I wanted to stand up, flip the table and then run around the cafe, pulling boardgames off the shelves and yelling, 'I can get a test!', then leap onto a bench and shower the room with Monopoly money.

'It's not cheap,' Libby went on, 'but it would be worth it.'

That was fine, I'd have Monopoly money.

'Of course it would. What does it involve?' I asked.

'All they would need to do,' she said, 'is take a sample of the amniotic fluid from the mother and test that along with a swab from you.'

'Okay.' I breathed in the information for a bit, assuming that amniotic fluid was a fancy term for what filled the baby's belly prison.

'Now,' Libby slowed her speech, 'it does come with some risks to the baby.'

'Like what?' I asked. The Monopoly money parade was now on hold.

'There is a very low chance that it could cause a miscarriage.'

I melted into the chair.

'Then it's definitely not happening.'

'It's super low risk,' she said. 'Like point zero…'

'There's no way that's even worth the risk. I'm not doing that,' I showed her how steady my eyes were. 'Tash wouldn't do it and I'd never ask.'

'It would give you an answer, that's all.' Libby leaned back.

The card game sat between us, far less complicated now. My head throbbed. Maybe this is why the game could go for up to thirty minutes. You had to account for moral dilemmas.

'What a fucking mess,' I said.

'You're right, it is a fucking mess.'

'Alright, calm down,' I shot back. She laughed for a second, then settled into a pensive stare. Her twitch hung around to keep us company.

'Libby, I have so much to think about right now. I don't really know how to process it. I definitely want a paternity test but not at the risk to the baby. I wouldn't do that to Tash. Like, I don't… I don't know.' I ran my palms over my face. 'I don't know anything.'

'I was just trying to think of solutions for you.'

Libby always had an intensity to what she said. Even if the suggestion was to try a new flavour of tea, she'd put it to you like an obligation. It made her commanding on stage. I loved watching her handle a heckler because her voice could cut them down before she even needed a punchline.

'I'm just not sure what to do before the kid is born,' I said.

'Hmm.' Libby swiped up the cards and began to fidget with them. 'Would you and Tash be together if there was no baby?'

My senses went numb. I was alone with Tash floating in front me, just out of reach. I'd move towards her but she drifted further into blackness. She didn't want to be around me. She just felt like she had to be.

'I guess not,' I said.

'Well then.' Libby shrugged. 'I'm sure you'll work out what to do.'

'Mate, I can't even work out how to play Flux.'

Libby's eye twitched again and she straightened the cards in her hands. They dropped back into the box and Libby stood up.

'In that case, I'll just get Uno.'

***

My phone sat on my desk, waiting for my decision. I walked back and forth in a half-circle around it, like I was about to start an interrogation. My lips made slight movements as I rehearsed lines about 'staying out of it' and 'waiting until the birth'. I clapped my hands a few times, and rubbed them together. *Alright, let's do this.* Instead of doing it, I left the bedroom and checked the fridge to confirm there was nothing edible in there. Back in the bedroom, I stared at the phone. This was the right thing to do. I avoided doing it by visiting the bathroom for the third time in twenty minutes.

The phone rang. My legs waddled me back into my room with my pants still unbuttoned.

It was Jin. I swore before answering.

'Yo.'

'Hey bro, I'm coming down to Melbourne next week for a few days. Can I crash at yours?'

I bit down on the impulse to say no. I *could* lie. Then there would be a whole new set of lies to come up with and I didn't have the brain space. Between that and the fact that I always stayed at his, the answer wasn't much of a choice.

'Yeah, man. Whatchu coming for?'

'Got some gigs and shit. Trying to get more serious with my stand-up.'

Sure he was.

'Great man. Just hit me up when you know what time you're coming in.'

'Thanks, bro. How's prego chick?' Jin said.

'She's good. We're going to get married.'

'For real?'

'Nope.'

'Ha! Yeah, don't get tied down, hey.'

'Thank you for the sage advice,' I said.

I told him I had to go live my life, then hung up. I saw I had missed a call from Tash. Fuck. She followed up with a text.

'Hey Ben, I know this is a lot to ask but are you coming to Perth any time soon? I don't want to do this all alone.'

12

I REREAD THE MESSAGE and crumbled onto the bed. My heart pounded as if I were running up a mountain. A sharp pain seared through the left side of my chest. *I'm having a heart attack!* The beating echoed through my bones. My back was drenched with sweat. *I'm dying! This is how people die!* I shot up and clutched at my heart. My breathing accelerated. Air sucked through my clenched teeth. I didn't know going into labour could happen this early…

I began to call the paramedics, then paused. I didn't have ambulance cover. *I'll just get an Uber to the hospital. Do I need the hospital?* The panic was escalating. I searched my contacts and found Zack's name. A puzzled voice answered.

'Ben?'

'Zack, I think I'm having a heart attack. What do I do? Should I go to the hospital? My heart is pounding, I can feel a sharp pain in my chest. I don't know what's happening.'

He adopted a stern voice like a hero would in a time of crisis. 'Take a deep breath, mate. Breathe out slowly.'

It helped.

'Just keep breathing nice and deep. Keep it slow,' he said. 'Now listen to me. You're in your twenties, you're not having a heart attack. You're having an anxiety attack. It can't hurt you so just calm down.'

I kept breathing deep. 'Okay. Are you sure? I'm pretty advanced for my age.'

'People having heart attacks aren't sarcastic. You're alright, mate. Tell me what's going on.'

Zack copped all the feelings, fears and the habitual sarcasm I couldn't restrain. He listened with the occasional 'hmm' and 'that must be hard' to my rant about Tash and money issues and how the smell of raw sausages stays on your skin even after a shower. It took somewhere between five-to-thirty minutes until my shoulders dropped and the adrenaline left my chest to make room for the feeling of unease.

'I'm sorry to call you. I didn't know what to do. I'm just so overwhelmed by everything right now.'

'It's okay, Tommo. Have you told your old man?'

Dad didn't know. My heart sped up again. What a day I was having. Was this how the human body had evolved? The Neanderthals who could withstand making the biggest fuck-ups could survive and thrive, while the weaklings like me would have their heart combust before they had a chance to procreate. Maybe I'd passed on my pathetic DNA to some poor kid before natural selection had a chance to pull me out of the gene pool.

'Ben?' I'm not sure what sound a furrowed brow makes but I swear I heard one come through the phone.

'Yes, ah yes,' I lied. 'Yeah, it's all good. I have people.' I tried to breathe deep without making it sound like I was addressing another panic attack.

'Life is a team sport, mate. You don't have to do it alone.'

'Thanks, Zack. I won't bug you again with this stuff.'

'It's totally okay,' he said it in a robotic enough tone for me to know not to bug him again. 'While I have you, and I hope this isn't too much to overload you with, but I did some asking around the hospital to find out more about paternity tests. They're not done here, you'll have to go through a DNA lab.'

My laptop was open before my next heartbeat.

Zack continued. 'There is, of course, a prenatal test that takes amniotic fluid from the mother, but I wouldn't recommend that in case it causes complications.'

'Right, yeah my friend told me that too. I'm just looking at a website now.'

The following options appeared on screen:

Peace of Mind Paternity Test:

- Highly Accurate
- DNA home kit arrives in the mail
- With or without the mother

$269

Legal Paternity Test:

- Valid in court
- We guide you through the paperwork
- Samples taken in-lab

$550

Prenatal Paternity Test (Risk-Free):

- Easy and Safe
- Sample taken from mother's blood after 9 weeks
- NB not recognised in Australian courts

$1490

My thumb tapped the desk. They were all such great options. One of each please. Legal, risk-free, peace of mind paternity test. I read them out to Zack and asked, 'What do they mean by the risk-free paternity test not being recognised in courts?'

'We only use the blood test method to screen for diseases in Australia. Not for paternity. I know the lab is trying to sell another product but they would be sending the samples offshore which is why Australian courts wouldn't recognise the results. It's a standards and practices issue.'

'I don't care about the courts. Can't we just do it and see what it says?' I said. 'I really just want to know anything at this point.'

'Look mate, I wouldn't trust that kind of test. The results could be inconclusive or just plain wrong.' He was firm. 'Do you really want to think you are the dad when you're not? Or the other way around?'

'I guess not.' My head hung in defeat.

'I can understand it's frustrating, mate, but if you don't get reliable results the mother or the other guy could take you to court and that risk-free test wouldn't mean shit. So whichever way you look at it, a prenatal test is off the table in my professional opinion.'

'Ah.' I lifted my head and dropped it again in double defeat.

'Look, Tommo,' his voice was one of a human's again, 'prenatal paternity tests are either risky or unreliable. It's up to you and the mother but I believe most doctors would recommend waiting until the child is born.'

'Mmm.' The laptop snapped shut.

'Are you going to be okay? How's your heart?' he asked.

'Still fast but I don't think I'm going to die in the next few minutes.'

'That's good. I have to go but take care, okay?'

'Thanks, Robbo.'

We hung up. My heart rate returned to normal after a while. I reopened my laptop to check my bank balance but then decided I didn't need an actual heart attack.

13

'OKAY, DAD I NEED TO tell you something,' I said into the wind, as I rode towards his place. My legs pedalled slow. The path wound downhill alongside the Merri Creek. Twisted trees and overgrown shrubs reflected in the brown water. The bike vibrated over the disfigured slats of a wooden bridge. I pulled over with a skid that would have looked cool if anyone were watching. This was the spot.

A five-year-old me and my sister Penny had wandered down to the creek in our gumboots. It was winter, but Melbourne never abided by the rules so the sun was out and the world was warm. We weren't meant to get this close to the creek. Dad had warned us not to go any further than the path but when we got there Penny said she just wanted to dip her feet in.

She ignored my feeble 'but Dad said…', flung off her boots and tiptoed into the stream. I followed with caution and stood at the bank as she waded further in until she was swimming.

'It's really nice!' she yelled at me, now treading water.

I yanked off a gumboot and eased my foot onto the soil. The mud slimed through my toes and made me flinch.

'It's gross!' I said.

'Leave your boots on then,' she called back.

I replaced the gumboot and slushed into the creek towards Penny. The water reached my hips, cold enough to shrink what was already small. The stream tugged me further in. Penny splashed at me. I tried to splash back but she swam further away, laughing as she chopped at the water.

On my next step forward, my waterlogged gumboots pulled me under the surface. I managed to kick one off but my panic became wild flailing. I kicked and kicked, trying to get the other boot off. It sank me down. My hands grasped at nothing, pulling through the water to no use. The light from above contorted in my vision. Everything faded. My limbs jerked in a final attempt to escape.

A hand found my collar and pulled. I curled my fingers around it and heaved myself upwards. My gaping mouth just made the air as Penny hooked her arms under mine and kicked us back to the bank. She dropped me onto the mud as I spluttered creek water out.

'You're an idiot!' she said. 'You are such an idiot.'

My bike wasn't moving but I crashed back to the present. This spot was where Penny had saved me so many years ago. The dull creek water flowed downstream like it didn't want to be anywhere near me. Typical. I kicked the pedal forward and got moving again.

About a kilometre from Dad's place the hills steepened and then levelled out to the main street. There was a shortcut through the laneways that branched behind the houses. It would require stopping to lift my bike onto the curb but I was ready to defy the laws of physics. They'd given me so much grief over the years. At full speed, I yanked my handlebars up to get lift but mistimed it. Bam. From my back on the pavement I could see my front wheel had warped. God. Damnit.

***

Penny's BMW was parked in front of Dad's place. It was white because she had no problem spending her dirty corporate money on regular car washes. My bike hadn't been cleaned since I had bought it. Now it wobbled next to me, begging me to go on without it.

Penny opened the door.

'Hey. What's happening?' she said without moving anything but her lower lip. A loud humming came from the back of the house. Dad was either angle grinding a slab of steel or flying a jet plane around the lounge room. I could guess the right answer but I chose to believe the wrong one to amuse myself.

'Not much, how you going?' I said.

'I'm good, just had a conference finish early today so popped in to visit. Dad's in the garden as always.'

Penny kept her hair cropped short, with blonde perfect highlights streaming through. It always seemed to hold the same shape when I saw her, every strand behaving itself as to not embarrass her in front of pretentious clientele. She wore a red velvet jacket over a puffy white shirt, a jade brooch pinned where the top button would be. Her phone case sparkled with golden glitter. That phone was always in her hand, ready to answer an email or serve as a mirror to keep an eye on her hair.

'Okay, I need to speak to him,' I said.

'Oh god, what's happened?'

'What makes you think something happened?'

'Since when do you come around just to chat to Dad?' she barked.

'I did the other day!'

'To eat his food, probably,' she said.

How dare she accuse me of the truth. 'Whatever.' I walked past her to the backyard.

Dad was using his hedge trimmers to groom the modest boxwood plant he had running along the flower bed. He wore a wide-brimmed hat, technicoloured sunglasses from the future and a face mask that he had no doubt kept well beyond its use.

'Dad!' I yelled. He didn't respond. He was trying to fix a dip in the hedge he'd created in lieu of hiring a professional.

I wound around to the other side of the hedge and waved. He flicked the switch off.

'Ben, son.' He pulled down his mask. 'Come to help?'

'Not quite. Can you come inside a minute? Just want to chat to you about something.' My voice portrayed enough urgency to get him to put the trimmers down.

Inside, Penny was at the dining room table typing something into her golden iPhone. It would have been easier to wait until she had left but my body was moving faster than my ability to plan. I took a chair opposite her and waited until Dad shuffled in. He was cupping something in his hand.

'I wanted to show you two, I found a dried-up centipede in the garden. Perfectly intact. Pretty impressive.' He eased it onto a placemat with his soft finger and admired it in the sunlight. I was sitting on my news, feeling it hopping around under me, ready to pounce out at everyone.

'I wonder how many legs it has,' Dad said. 'Did you know that they never have an even amount of legs? It's always an odd number. Any guesses before I count?'

'Dad, I was told by someone I slept with that she's now pregnant but we don't know if I'm the dad.'

Penny looked up at me for a second and then back down at her screen, shaking her head. 'You're an idiot'.

'Thanks for your support. Look, I just want to know if I can borrow some money to head to Perth for a bit to sort things out with the mother and support her.'

'Who are you asking? Me or Dad?' said Penny.

Dad was eyeing his garden discovery and stroking his brow with his thumb.

'Dad mainly, but I'll take anything at this point,' I said.

'How far along is she?' Penny pressed me, lowering her device.

'Just over twelve-ish weeks, I think.'

'Who is she? When were you in Perth?' she asked.

'About ten weeks ago. Look, pregnancy dating is complicated.'

'Dad?' Penny turned to him for aid in the interrogation. Dad was now looking out the window, his face dull and sombre. He took a long breath in and let it out as slow as a human could manage.

'How likely is it to be yours?' he asked, keeping his eyes outside.

My teeth found a bit of dry skin on my lip and chomped at it until it came off. It was the first thing I'd eaten all day. I told them everything I knew.

Penny swore as she exhaled. Dad looked down at the centipede again.

'Well,' she said, 'Dad doesn't have the money.'

'He can speak for himself,' I said. Dad kept admiring the dry bug, spinning it around with his index finger.

'I am speaking for him,' said Penny, 'because I'm paying his bills and buying his food.'

'Since when!?'

'Do you want to tell him?' She turned to Dad.

'Tell me what?' I asked.

Dad kept playing with the centipede until the tension reached a critical mass.

'I had a little issue with the pokies,' he said.

'What are you, eighty-years-old?' I asked. 'Why are you playing the pokies?'

'That's not important now.' Penny wove her fingers together and placed them on the table, assuming the posture of a movie villain revealing their master plan.

'How much did you lose?' I stared at Dad. My whole body tightened. My chair was about to be swallowed up by all the clenching.

Penny kept her sights on Dad, Dad kept his on the centipede, the centipede avoided all eye contact.

'How much did you lose, Dad?' I asked again.

'A bit. Well, a lot.' He paused. 'Pretty much all my savings.'

I buried my face in my hands and attempted to rearrange my features so I would fit into a different family.

'So what does this mean?' I spoke into my wrists. It was a question that had a more specific question within it: *what does this mean for me?* I'd been walking a financial tightrope for years. Now I was being told that the safety net had been chopped up and fed into a pokie machine. Within the second question was another one I didn't even want to address right now: *how does this make me feel about Dad?* I'd long outgrown the idea that he was infallible but I hadn't realised that a man's flaws could cast a shadow over his kids.

Maybe mine would too.

Penny tilted her poreless face at me. There might have been a real human under it but I wasn't going to make any more assumptions today.

'It means,' she said, the faintest smirk forming on her lips, 'that you need to get a job.'

14

LYGON STREET IN MELBOURNE is known as *Little Italy*. It should be known as *A Little of Everything*. It started out as a strip of Italian restaurants run by first and second-generation Italian immigrants. By 2017 it was much more eclectic with hipster cafes, Thai restaurants, kebab joints and burger franchises. The Carlton end of the street had kept a majority of Italian places, but only just. The restaurants retained the long-standing tradition of having a waiter on the street persuading people walking by to come dine at their particular establishment for a free glass of wine. Couples and groups were prime targets of this aggressive charm. A lone, dishevelled young man such as me was never bothered by these waiters. Their Euro-Australian accents were better spent on people who dressed like they could afford more than a glass of water.

It was a Sunday afternoon. A dark, cloudy sky lay over the world, indifferent to my problems, as I walked down Lygon towards the main stretch of Italian joints. I was holding a manilla folder with a dozen copies of my resume. My employment history felt light. The first stop on my hunt was *La Donnetta*. The building was painted white, with a shop front of tall glass panels. At 4 p.m. there was only a handful of customers scattered around the outside tables. A tall blond guy with a red cap and white shirt hovered in front of the door with his arms behind his back and a black apron around his waist. He was daydreaming until I approached and snapped him back to his job.

'Table for one, sir?' he said in a modern German accent. The kind that was modelled off American rap music but still retained a robotic cadence.

'No, actually,' I said. 'I was wondering if there are any jobs going.'

'I will get the manager.'

The German guy spun on his heels and went inside. The window had a yellowing sign peeling off it reading, 'Help Wanted'. It looked as if they had put it up when the shop first opened and just left it there. It was surrounded by framed Ferrari merchandise: photos, t-shirts and caps. Wherever there were gaps between those, there was an Italian flag or a picture of some *very* Italian people. The decor overwhelmed me but the smell of pizza kept me in place long enough to wait for the manager.

A short Middle Eastern-looking man walked out with the German guy following. He was wearing a black apron with finger marks of flour all over it and a gold chain that had the Lebanese tree hanging off it. He was either from there or was just really into trees.

'You want job?' he said.

'Yes, I have had some waitering experience when I was about sixteen…' I began to fish out a resume.

'Okay, you come back for a trial tomorrow. Six o'clock.'

'Alright. Yes, awesome. Thanks,' I said.

'What's your name?'

'I'm Ben Thomas.' I shook his hand.

'I'm Ali. Okay, Ben, you come tomorrow. Bleck shoes, bleck pants.'

'Cool. See you then.'

Ali disappeared inside. The German guy resumed his position then directed his attention to a couple strolling past. He stepped forward but before he could start his spiel, the woman pointed at me.

'Are you that comedian?' she asked, her eyes wide open. She wore a purple peacoat that wrapped tight around her torso so that the buttons were strained. Her bright red beanie matched the hue of her big round cheeks.

'I'm one of many comedians,' I said.

'We saw you at the Lounge the other week. Very funny.' She pulled at her partner's arm to get his acknowledgement.

'Yeah, you were great,' he said. He was all legs and a pair of glasses. His black Hard Rock Cafe t-shirt was visible under a studded leather jacket. She must have picked him up at a vintage store or gone back in time to when those clothes were affordable.

'Thank you. That's really sweet of you.' I couldn't offer them a direct look. It felt as though I had almost been busted for cheating on an exam. From their limited view, I was a real-life comedian. Not an unemployed person who sometimes gets paid for his hobby.

'Are you a comedian?' The German was puzzled.

'Ah, yeah.' It was painful to say.

'Then why do you need a job here?'

I wondered if the Ferrari scarf in the window could be used to strangle a man.

'You're looking for work?' The woman asked. I whipped the folder of resumes behind my back despite knowing she'd seen it already.

'Oh no,' I said. 'I was just…'

'But you just asked for a job.' German guy tilted his head at me.

I bit down on my tongue but only because I couldn't get to his. He squinted like an alien trying to understand why humans blew out the candles on their birthday cake after having just lit them. Don't question these things, German guy. It's just how society works.

'Yeah well,' I said. 'I was… I was just doing it for the, um.'

Ali reappeared and approached the couple, flapping a menu at them.

'You want to eat? We have beautiful pasta for you,' he said.

'We're fine thanks, we were just going.' The purple coated woman started down Lygon Street but before she could get any further an obese man with greasy, slicked-back hair accosted her partner with a bouquet of roses.

'Sir, buy a rose for your lady?' He asked.

'This guy is a comedian.' The German guy was now telling Ali.

'Comedian? Tell me joke then,' Ali said.

'Er, no thank you.' The leather jacket guy said to the rose salesman, raising his palms in defence. The purple peacoat lady's cheeks were redder than ever.

'I have to…' I began to say.

'Just one rose! Only eight dollars, my friend.'

'No really, thank you.' The woman said.

'I have to go,' I told Ali. 'Sorry.' It was meant for everyone. I darted off, not quite knowing where to head. When I turned the corner I gathered speed, past the restaurants, scraggy residential fences and into the park. Behind a row of trees, there was a free bench. My breath caught up. The folder turned over in my fingers. It was bent from scrunching it in my fist when I ran. I twisted it even more and threw it at a nearby bin, missing and making the pages fall everywhere. *I'm not going to be a fucking waiter.*

***

'I should have been a fucking waiter,' I said to Jin as I stepped into my apartment. It was dark outside now and my living room was as bright as the last working light bulb could manage.

'Why? Haven't you been getting many gigs?' he asked. His backpack was on the floor. A lifetime-supply of v-neck shirts spilled out onto the carpet. He was reclining on the couch, scrolling through his phone. My guess was that he was ogling hot girls on Instagram.

'Nah, I've had other shit on,' I said, facing away. I opened the cupboard above the stove, hoping there was something edible in it. There were a few cans of assorted boring food and empty packets of more exciting treats.

'How's the baby stuff?' he asked.

'It's fine. I'll find out if it's mine when it's born.'

'Why can't you find out sooner?'

Well, Jin, it's because the prenatal test has a zero point five percent chance of causing a miscarriage, which could mean Tash loses the baby and even though those odds are super low, especially because we're in Australia and our medical technology is pretty advanced, there is no way I am going to suggest it to her in the event that the worst-case scenario happens, so now I can't make any life decisions until I know what my obligations are and I don't have any money to go to Perth to be there with her so fuck off out of my apartment you v-neck wearing dickhead.

'It's complicated.' I shrugged.

Jin sucked at his tongue and tutted for a bit. His coconut fake tan overpowered the lingering Garden Escape.

'Someone from A-List saw me last night,' he said.

'What?' I tried to steady my voice halfway through the word.

'Yeah my friend knows the main guy there.' He shrugged now. 'I thought it couldn't hurt for them to see me.'

I could hurt him though. Not for long. Flipping the couch over and pinning him underneath might work. Then he wouldn't be able to do any gigs. Then I could do all the gigs. Then I would be seen by A-List and make money and visit Perth and buy a house and never let Jin come over.

'That's cool, man. Congrats.' I sized up the couch. Whatever reason I'd had to let Jin stay over had long abandoned me. He lazed over the cushions with his dumb muscles. He was about to say something but then just yawned.

I tipped a can of beans into a bowl and heated them for half the ideal time. A taste test revealed a mix of cold and way-too-hot beans. They would do. I started towards my room when Jin spoke up again.

'Ben?'

'Yo.'

'I think A-List is going to sign me.'

I choked on a hot bean. The top of my mouth got burnt and the coughing gave me a reason to hide my reaction to his news.

'Ouch, hot. Sorry. Great, man, that's great.'

'Yeah, it's crazy hey? We should get smashed to celebrate.'

'Not tonight, man. I've got some stuff to do.' That 'stuff' was avoiding throwing the bowl of baked beans through the window. If I threw it hard enough maybe it would make it to Lygon Street and hit the German guy.

'I'll speak to you in the morning,' I said, closing my bedroom door behind me.

'Alright, bro. G'night,' Jin said before it shut.

My laptop speakers blared to max. The music covered the sound of my punches into the pillow. I fumed across the carpet, scratching at sheets of notebook paper and throwing them towards the plastic bag. The red chair toppled over under my swift kick. My reflection in the bedroom window was grumpy. I didn't need a guy like that around so I shut the blinds with a sharp tug of the string. Too hard. The force pulled the whole blind frame off the screws. It fell onto the bowl of beans sitting on the bedside table and catapulted them all over the carpet. A four-letter word bounded out of my lips.

There was a knock at the bedroom door.

'Bro!' Jin said through the wood. I didn't respond. Instead, I flicked the light off, removed my shoes and squished over baked beans to get into bed.

'Bro!' He pushed the door open and stepped in. Little did he know there was a boobie trap of legumes waiting for him if he came any closer. My arm covered my face. It was a trick I'd learned as a child to hide from monsters and getting in trouble.

'What's going on, man? I'm worried about you,' he said.

'It's nothing,' I said. 'I'm going to sleep.'

The light came on.

'It's something.' Jin said. 'Is it the prego chick?'

'Yes, Jin. It's the prego chick. And it's my fucked career. And it's my empty bank account. And it's the bowl of beans. It's everything. I've messed everything up.'

'Bro.'

'All I want to do right now is see Tash. That's the prego chick. I want to talk to her and look after her. But she's in Perth. I have no money to go see her. I have no money to do anything.'

'Bro!' He stretched the word out to span the length of the room. 'That sucks.'

'I tried to get a job tonight at a restaurant but I can't do it. I just can't do it, man. What if I get a gig? Am I going to quit a restaurant job and then need to find another one the next day?' I answered my own questions with a groan.

'When do you have to go to Perth?' he said.

'She's not going to be pregnant forever, so as soon as I can.'

'I can spot you. I got mad cash from my parents.'

I sat up fast. The beans were now floating around the bed. They brushed over my legs as I moved.

'I'm not borrowing money from you, Jin.'

'Why?'

Because I've been imagining hurting you and kicking you out of my apartment. Your act of kindness would make me feel like a total arsehole and I'm not giving you the satisfaction.

'It's complicated,' I said.

Jin pulled out his phone. He stood just in from the doorway, tapping at the screen without saying a word. The soft light behind him created a glow around his beach-ready body. My phone beeped.

'There, it's done,' he said. 'I just sent five hundred bucks to you. Stay at my place when you're there.'

'Wait, what? How?' A notification on my screen said a transfer had been made.

'You can do it using people's phone number now. Just accept it, bro. I got cash, don't worry.'

'No, Jin, really I can't.'

'Go to Perth, my man. You'll make sick money one day and you can pay me back.'

'Right, but I'm not even sure it's my baby…'

'Do you like this chick?' Jin asked.

'Well, yeah.'

'Then you're doing the right thing, bro.'

My mouth hung open. Not so much because of Jin's kindness but more at the wisdom coming from a brain eroded by so many dexis. Jin left me to lie in my shock and baked beans. I looked at my phone again. The notification was still there like a caring friend. The beans grew cold before I could bring myself to believe it.

I retrieved my laptop from under some shirts but then hesitated. Tash came to mind. She wore her purple lipstick under the nightclub lights and stood on the dance floor holding a child in her delicate arms. I approached her as blurs of people stumbled around us. The baby was crying, reaching out to me. I held it and gave it comfort. It calmed and fell asleep. The scene around me faded to black. All the advice from Libby, Penny and Jin faded with it, leaving me alone holding a child. My child.

In the reality of my dusty room, my fingers found the search bar and bought a flight to my least favourite place in the world.

15

'CAN YOU HOLD THIS for me?' Tash handed me her pink tote bag and vanished behind the fitting room door.

Next to me, three other men stood in a line with their backs against the wall, all holding various handbags belonging to their invisible counterparts. There was solidarity in our awkwardness. Not that any of them acknowledged me, I just knew we were bros.

'I'm a whale,' Tash said from inside the cubicle.

'I like whales,' I replied. One of the men turned to me. He was wearing a burgundy floral shirt that he for sure didn't pick for himself. He shook his head, showing terror in his wide eyes.

'I mean, you're not a whale, Tash,' I corrected myself. 'You're a powerful childbearing woman.'

Floral shirt gave me a thumbs up.

The door groaned open a fraction. A sliver of Tash's face appeared in the gap. Heavy foundation covered the insecurities that had popped up on her skin in the last week. Hormones are so unfair on people. Enough of her lips were visible to betray a frown.

'Can I see?' I said.

'No.'

'Okay.'

'Fine, come in.' She disappeared again but left the door ajar.

Tash's tight white top was tucked into the jeans she was trying on. The waistband had patches made from a stretchy material where the pockets would have been. They allowed her swollen belly to push out above them. She flopped her arms down next to her to assert her mood.

'It's only meant to be an avocado right now,' she said.

My eyebrows expressed my bemusement.

'Haven't I shown you the app yet?' Tash fished out her phone from the tote bag and opened up a pregnancy calendar app. It had a series of fruits and vegetables indicating the size of a foetus at different stages during the pregnancy. Last week it was an apple. This week: an avocado.

'Aren't avocados known for having good fats?' I asked.

I heard a deliberate cough from outside. Tash pouted and turned away.

'You look beautiful,' I said. 'You're growing a human in there. Don't be so hard on yourself.'

'Oh my god!' Tash spun around to face me, pressing her palms to her stomach. 'I just felt it kick!

The cubicle door flew open to my unglamorous support team. 'We just felt the baby kick!' I said.

'Congrats dude!' Flower man said. The other two weren't sure how to react but offered faint grins. Two women peered out of their fitting rooms to find the source of the commotion.

'Oh my god!' became a contagious phrase as Tash presented the swelling avocado. The women touched her belly, without asking, with such glee that the thrill of the moment overtook everyone. Whether it was the fluorescent lighting or the pure excitement from her own body, Tash was incandescent. Our new friends chatted with her in heightened voices about how far along she was, how she's been feeling and so on. She giggled and blushed as she downplayed her pains and woes.

I took a step back, not knowing if it was really my place to share such a moment. I was either bonding with my future family or just setting myself up for sadness.

Floral shirt man approached me and slapped my shoulder. It was the masculine way of conveying pride, sympathy and bruises.

'Not long now, hey? You'll be changing nappies before you know it.'

'I'm not worried,' I said, 'I wear them myself.'

He laughed like it was the first time he had been allowed to in years.

***

'Where are you staying?'

We were walking through the outside strip of the Murray Street Mall, in between the large chain stores and public buildings. The busy foot traffic kept our pace slow as we let people weave around us. They shuffled by with much more certainty about where their lives were going. A Lorna Jane store was opposite Lululemon, both competing for Tash's attention and desire for overpriced activewear. She was already carrying a shopping bag with two pairs of the stretchy jeans.

'Down the other end of Hay Street,' I replied, pulling my sight away from the model on the giant Lorna Jane poster before Tash saw and I had to pretend like I was admiring the font or something. Not that we were involved in any romantic way, it just seemed rude not to squash my single-life habits.

'At like a hotel?' she asked.

'I'm actually staying at my friend Jin's apartment. He's at my place in Melbourne right now so it's a fair trade.'

'When is he back?' She stopped in front of speckled grey gym pants in the Lululemon window.

'In about a week,' I said.

Tash mentioned something about the gym pants but I was consumed with analysing her questions. She was either just starting conversation or probing to see if she could come over. It was a risky game guessing someone's intention. The easiest and most mature solution would be to just say 'why do you ask?' and push for a direct response.

'Yeah those pants are cool,' I said instead, hoping it was a valid reply to whatever she had just said.

We ambled further down the mall towards a busker playing an Ed Sheeran cover. His man bun was tied up in a haphazard way that let a few strands of hair fall over his face, annoying me more than it appeared to do to him. He had a loop pedal set up next to a boom mic stand, behind his open acoustic guitar case. Inside, a cardboard sign had his Instagram handle written on it. It stood over a dozen or so silver and gold coins. Under some of the coins were ten- and twenty-dollar notes that I'm sure no audience member placed there. The busker, or @TomBoyMusicPerth, had a strong voice and a sweet strum of the guitar but it was a common trick for buskers to put notes in their case from their own pocket to make larger donations seem not unprecedented.

Tash tapped my shoulder with her knuckle and flicked her chin towards TomBoyMusicPerth.

'He's dope!' she said.

There was some change in the coin pocket of my jeans. Only a couple of twenty-cent coins but I jingled them in my fist to give off that high roller vibe. I crouched down near the case and threw them in where a lot of other coins were to cover their identity. Despite my effort to conceal the contribution, Tash noticed it was light.

She beckoned me back and reached for my hand. Leading me in the opposite direction, she pointed to a mannequin in the Zara window. It appeared male but I was woke enough not to assume its pronouns. The mannequin wore a tan corduroy jacket with woollen lining. Even the plastic figure looked comfortable in it.

'You'd look great in that. The tan matches your skin tone,' she said.

'Thank you, I try to keep my pasty look going year-round.'

'Let's go try it on.'

'That's alright,' I said. 'I'm saving my money for a Lorna Jane outfit.'

'Come on, Mr Comedian.' She giggled.

Tash stepped into the white glow of the store and I followed. We found a jacket in my size. It was a bit tight around the shoulders, which I liked because it made me feel buff for a change.

'It looks great!' Tash flipped the back of the collar up to give me more style than I was qualified for. I snuck a glance at the price tag and tried to calculate how long to leave it on to make it appear like I was considering buying it.

'Hmm, yeah it's alright,' I said.

'I'm going to get it for you.'

'Oh no, please. I have money, I just…'

'I know, but you spent money to come to Perth just to check on me. Don't think I don't see you. I asked and you came. And gift-giving is my love language.'

'Love language? Does that mean…' I didn't finish the sentence so she could complete it for me.

'I don't mean…' she blushed. 'It's just a term to explain how people show their affection. For some people, their love language is touch. Others it's acts of service. For me, it's gift-giving and I just want to show you I'm grateful you came to visit. You didn't have to. So let me buy it?'

She swung her bags around so she could find her purse. Seeing her happy for the first time since this whole pregnancy thing kicked off brought such relief. It would be rude of me to deny her the cheer. Plus the jacket had now been warmed by my body heat and we had a good thing going on.

When we left Zara, Tash was almost skipping. There was a new bounce to my step too. Fashion could make you so buoyant.

'How's study going?' I asked. 'Are you still doing classes?'

'Yeah! I'm loving it. We just started the practised-research unit where we make something that we study the history of. I wanted to do a wrap dress, partly because it's a perfect pregnancy dress but also because it was made famous by my absolute favourite designer, Diane von Fürstenberg. Oh my god, she is my spiritual guide. I bet you if I showed you some of her original designs even you would recognise them. So seventies.'

She said all this without taking air in. Learning new things about Tash after so many weeks made me smile. There was so much to respond to and some of the terms were beyond me but that didn't matter. She was sharing.

'That sounds cool!' I meant it. 'What's a wrap dress?'

'It's a dress that you wrap.' She made herself laugh. 'That's the simple explanation anyway.'

We strolled past shopfronts and around corners. Tash told me about how Diane von Fürstenberg got into fashion because she didn't want to just be a rich housewife to a German prince. But then it was funny because later she got divorced and her ex-husband decided to get into fashion. Tash enjoyed the theory that her hero, Diane, made the wrap dress because she used to complain that zips were too noisy to put on the morning after a hook-up when trying to sneak out. Turns out I could relate.

It wasn't until the salty cloud of McDonald's oil hit us that I knew where we'd wandered to.

'Ah, we're on Hay Street,' I said. 'My place is just down there.' It was meant to be a comment but it landed like a suggestion.

'Great, can I use your bathroom? I need to pee so bad.'

'Um, yeah sure. It's just another five minutes this way if you can hold on that long. Or I think this McDonald might have one.' I tacked on the last part to be nonchalant. She could come around. Whatever. No biggie here. The day had been great so far, though, and why wouldn't we keep hanging out? We were getting along and that could only be a desirable quality in potential co-parents/partners/lovers.

'I can definitely wait,' she said. She must have felt the same.

When we got there, Tash went to the bathroom straight away. She then wandered around, tilting Jin's possessions as if assessing their value. I offered her water, as that was the only liquid in the place besides alcohol and human growth hormone.

'Thanks,' she said. 'And can I ask you something?'

'Yes?' I placed her water near her on the kitchen bench and then leaned against it to capture that cool pose I was famous for.

'Did you come to Perth for me or the child?'

Something in my chest swelled. It pushed out against my rib cage to the point I was expecting to hear a crack.

'Ah,' I stammered. Instead of considering the true thing to say, my brain processed the options of the funniest thing to say. *I'm just here for that winter beach weather.* Nope. *We're in Perth!? I thought this was Guantanamo.* No. I couldn't decide on anything so I delivered the truth. 'I'm here because you said you couldn't do this alone. And, you know, if the other guy isn't involved then I guess… I guess it's not good for you or the child to go through a tough time without support. So both?'

She nodded and sipped her water. She nodded again, offering no response, so I continued.

'My dad raised me. All on his own. He was there even when everything went to shit for him. I'd like to think I could do the same for my kid.' I met her soft gaze. 'Have you told your parents yet? You surely have other people to support you too.'

'I'll level with you, Ben.' She put the glass back down as if she was no longer allowed to have it. 'It's really only you, the other guy and my doctor who know at the moment. I've been way too scared to even imagine what my parents would think of me if I told them I was pregnant and I didn't know who the father was.'

It was just as well she hadn't told them. She might find out they had a gambling problem or some other shocking revelation parents liked doing these days.

'When are you going to tell them?' I asked.

'Not till I have to. Which could be soon… I might have to move out of my place.'

'Why?'

'It's complicated,' she sighed. Ah, yes, 'complicated'. The best word to cover the real answer.

'Stay here.' I gestured.

The words came from somewhere. It seemed to be my mouth but I didn't remember asking it to say anything.

'That's very sweet, Ben. But it's already getting a bit confusing with everything.'

'Then let me clear things up,' I said. 'I'll sleep on the couch, you can take the bed. Totally fine. I promise it won't be weird. And that will at least give you a little more time to find an alternative.'

'You don't have…'

'Hey, you didn't have to get me this jacket. Let's just say that supporting the mother of my potential child through a confusing paternal crisis is my love language.'

Tash's snort-laugh vibrated through the whole apartment. She came closer and gave me a hug. It was tight and warm, and her belly pressed to mine enough to feel the avocado inside it kick.

16

'PUT YOUR HANDS TOGETHER, make some noise, give me some whoops and cheers and welcome to the stage Bernie Colman!'

The crowd filled every seat at Shapiro Tuesdays. There were almost ninety people and the booze in them had turned their cheers into war cries. My hands pumped the air to rally these beer-filled soldiers of mirth. As Bernie appeared in the stage doorway behind me, I adjusted the mic stand to his height of crazy tall and then hustled backstage.

Eight or so of society's oddest collection of dorks chilled on couches and the floor of a half-office, half-storage room. The energy from the crowd in the theatre still leaked through the brick wall separating us. I perched myself on the armrest of the faded brown couch and read over the running order I'd scribbled out on the back of an envelope.

'Dawit Abebe?' I asked the room.

'That's me.' An African-looking guy on the other side of the room flicked his head at me. He appeared fresh out of high school and was dressed like he had a job interview nowhere more pretentious than McDonald's: a button-up shirt and a pair of formal shoes he might have borrowed from his dad. He had his notebook out and was leaning into it as if proximity to the page helped with memorisation.

'Sweet man, you're next. Did I say it right?' He gave me a nod and a shrug at the same time. I smiled, ready to ask him to say it right for me but then accepted that he would have spent enough energy over the course of his life trying to make the nasal Australian accent bend its jagged edges around his native pronunciation. Instead, I clicked my tongue and gave him the okay sign with my fingers.

The room booker, Sarah, was next to me. Her sandy brown hair was pulled tight in a ponytail and her foot was tucked under her bum. She was mid-conversation with a comic in a baby blue Stussi cap and a beard that would have taken real commitment to grow so neglected.

'But that's it, isn't it?' Sarah continued. 'All the real gigs are in Melbourne.'

'Totally,' said beard man.

'This pays better than a Melbourne gig,' I chipped in.

'Right, but there are way less gigs. Plus there's no TV here. And no agents. How many times can you do Shapiro's in a year, you know?'

'True.' I turned the running order over in my fingers.

'Yeah,' the beard guy agreed. 'I'll probably head over for Comedy Fest next year and see how that goes before making the move.' He had such a low voice I had to lean in to make out his words. That made me slip sideways from the armrest and throw my hand onto Sarah's knee for balance.

'Oops, shit sorry.'

'All good.' She turned back to beard boy. 'I'll definitely go a bit beforehand just to get settled. My job is letting me transfer so I may as well go in January.'

Beardy bro turned to me and asked, 'Have you done it?'

'The festival? Yeah, I do it every year,' I said.

'That's crazy. A new show every year?' Sarah joined in.

'Yeah.'

'Damn, how do you write that fast? I'm struggling to get twenty minutes,' she said.

'Just hope shit happens to you and go from there,' I responded, looking back down at the running order to remember the next comedian's name. 'Also club material is different to festival material. In a room like this or The Comic's Lounge you have to crush as hard as possible. In a show that's your own, for an hour, you can have what I call "festival minutes". I'd never do that material in a club but in a solo show people are more willing to go along for the ride without as many laughs. More stories and personal stuff.'

'Yeah, I've heard other people mention that,' Hairy McHair Face said.

'I might not do it next year though,' I said.

'Why not?' Sarah asked, pulling her hair tie off, placing it in her mouth and redoing her ponytail.

'I might be moving to Perth.'

'You got a job here?' she asked.

'Not yet.'

'Partner?'

'It's complicated.' I stood up to end the conversation I knew I was responsible for starting. 'Has he got the light yet?' The stage door peep-hole was installed the wrong way. A microscopic version of Bernie still had the mic in his hand and the stand was off to the side. There was enough of a gap in the wall to put my ear to. Bernie was at punchline.

'So then I said, "Yeah, fifty bucks motherfucker!"' The audience howled.

Dawit joined me at the stage door. He was pacing a bit, muttering to himself while inspecting his shoes and making nervous gestures.

'They're a great crowd, you'll have a good time,' I said.

'Yeah cool, cool.' He scratched his scalp with all ten fingers. 'This is only like my third gig.'

'Dude, you'll be great. Have fun.'

Bernie announced his departure loud enough to muffle through the door. I swung it open to see him in front of the mic stand, one hand raised in the air after a glorious victory. We shook hands as we passed by each other.

'One more time for Bernie!' I said. The mic stand adjusted to my height under a twist of my wrist. 'Before I bring out your next act, I was thinking about babies. Anyone here got a kid?' No answer. 'Fair enough. Though I have a feeling that might change after tonight you sexy mofos. I know what you get up to after comedy shows.' The drunkest audience members cheered.

'But anyway, I was thinking about how couples always want to find out a baby's gender before it's born. Why? I want an ultrasound that can tell me the kid's IQ.' I beamed at the stupid idea. 'Gender doesn't matter, let's be honest. But it would be pretty handy to know if you're getting a Stephen Hawking or a Forrest Gump.' The response was promising.

'Personally,' I went on, 'I want my kid to have the lowest IQ possible. I just think it's important for kids to be able to relate to their father.' Boom. The audience broke out in fits. That was a keeper. Plus the butt of the joke was me, so I wouldn't have to field any angry comments about disparaging low intelligence. Dancing around offence was always the most fun.

'Alright, let's get the applause back up. Come on! Keep it going for your next act, Dawit Abebe.' I signalled for the crowd to clap louder before I said his name. It helped cover any mispronunciation on my part. Dawit arrived with a handshake. He trembled in my grip so I gave him a pat on the back before returning to the green room. He was me so many years ago.

'I'm going to try watch,' Bernie said and strode toward the show-room entrance.

'He's awesome,' Sarah said to me. 'Very new but I reckon he could win Raw next year.'

'Yeah? I'll go watch then.' I followed where Bernie had gone, down the hallway and towards the audience entrance. He was leaning against the doorway where you could see the stage front-on. I gave him a nod and tilted my head to see in. Dawit had his arm stretched out like he had just finished karate chopping the air. He yelled into the mic with the energy of a whole rock band.

'My dad doesn't know how to use his iPad! He buys all the latest, most expensive ones! And then two weeks later my mum is using them as coasters!'

He needed to move the mic stand to the side to get it out of the line of sight to him, get rid of his bouncing leg, not yell every single punchline and engage the back of the room. Other than that he was a natural. The room loved him and rewarded him with enough laughs to make any teenager feel like a god. I remembered that feeling and missed it.

'People ask me where I'm from all the time! I tell them that where I'm from is super dangerous! Wild animals are everywhere! Crime rates are through the roof! It's a third world country!' He paused to perfection. 'I'm from Mandurah.' The crowd erupted in howls and claps.

'Where's that?' I asked Bernie in a whisper.

'It's the shit suburb.'

'Ah.'

'Yeah, man!' Dawit's chest puffed out. 'When I apply for jobs, I don't put my name Dawit Abebe on the CV! I just put a photo of a white guy on it and mail it in! And if they ask me about it when I turn up for the job interview, I just say my printer was out of ink!'

Dawit began to strut around the stage with increasing intensity: impersonating his dad and dipping in and out of accents. His face was so animated it brought us glee with just a goofy expression. I was so engrossed that when he grabbed the mic stand to finish his set, Bernie had to prod me into remembering there was a job to do. Instead of bolting for the backstage entrance, I only had time to charge down the aisle and take the mic back from there. Dawit was pure elation and waved to the crowd instead of seeing my outstretched hand. He left the stage, leaving me to mime a handshake to steal a laugh from the gaff.

When the show was over and Sarah had handed me my envelope of a hundred and fifty dollars in curled yellow notes. A few comics reclined on the couches letting the buzz of the night evaporate from their bodies.

'You killed tonight, dude,' I told Dawit, who was sitting on the corner of the couch opposite me. His knee was hopping up and down, raring to get in front of another crowd no doubt.

'Thanks man! You're from Melbourne yeah?'

'Yep,' I said.

'Have you ever done the Gala?'

My stomach jolted. Perhaps it was the baby kicking. The Comedy Festival Gala had always been a mirage that moved further away the more I pursued it. It stood alone as the biggest validation a comic could have in this country. Even Australia's Jim Jeffries, who went on to get his own Comedy Central show in America, snag a bunch of Netflix specials and sell out stadiums all over the world, was rumoured to lament never getting a spot on the Gala. It was like slaying a dragon without getting a knighthood.

'No, I did ABC *Comedy Up Late* last year.' That was the diet coke of the Gala. My set got a lot of views online too, but whoever was in charge of social media had forgotten to put my name on the post. A lot of the comments just asked who the hell I was and listed comedians they liked more.

'That's sick! How did you get that?' Dawit asked.

'Er, just, you know, gigs and stuff.'

'I can't wait. I want to get into Raw so bad.'

'You could do it, my dude. Even just getting into the National Finals is sick.'

'I wanna win,' he said. 'And I want to get into Comedy Zone the next year.'

'Easy tiger. One gig at a time.' This was the same advice I had ignored when I was coming up. Dawit continued to ask excited questions about the industry, money, and other things he didn't realise I sucked at. His frantic intensity made me feel inspired, envious and sombre all at once.

'A few of us are going to The Moon to eat if anyone else wants to come,' Sarah put to us.

'You coming?' Dawit asked, leaping to his formal shoes.

'I would but I got to go live my life,' I said.

The others scoffed at me in fake offence and said their goodbyes.

'Nice to meet you, dude,' Dawit said and then left with the others. He was striding towards a life of TV appearances, awards, sold-out theatres and direct messages from cute girls on Instagram. What an arsehole.

***

The front door of Jin's apartment closed under my soft press. The kitchen light was on and empty souvlaki bags were still on the bench, wet and crumpled. The bedroom door was left open. A blue light from the TV flickering over a resting Tash.

'How was the gig?' she called out.

'Good,' I said, not feeling like recounting how much better it was for Dawit. 'Want me to close the door?'

'Come hang out for a bit. I can't sleep anyway.'

The bed was pushed up to the window and she was lying on the accessible side. I crawled under the doona from the bottom of the bed, popping up onto the one pillow left for me out of the four. My bum cheek discovered the remote to the TV and informed my hand so it could turn it down. Tash told me about cramps and aches she'd had, then about trying to finish her fashion portfolio, and her plan to ask her friend Krystal if she could stay with her for a while. My nods and assurances calmed her. She fell asleep half-way through an episode of *Friends*.

It would be inappropriate to sleep next to her but rude to wake her by trying to get out of the bed. It took an hour of staring out the window before I accepted that sleep didn't want to get involved anyway.

After midnight, a Facebook message came in from someone named Todd Kershaw. From the profile photo, I saw that my friend thought 'Power' would be a more magical stage name. It sure was.

'Hey buddy, Todd Power from the A-List showcase here. I'm back in Aus to do a few shows at the Opera House in two weeks. I've put your name forward to open for me, I want someone super different from me and I think you'd be perfect. You around?'

The sheets were almost pulled clean off Tash as I sat up fast. She groaned.

'Ben?'

'Sorry, sorry!' I said.

'Are you okay?'

'I'm fine. Keep sleeping.'

She sighed, recovered herself in the sheets and fell quiet again. She appeared to be a sleeping woman. Not a pregnant woman. Not a damsel in need of my constant rescue. Not a wife or even my girlfriend.

Natasha Peters would be fine at her friend's place with the care of her doctor not too far away. If she needed, she had parents, family and the whole internet for endless access to other confused pregnant women. The delivery day was far off too. Until then, I would just be floating around her becoming more confused as to my role in her life.

My teeth bit into my cheek and I typed back to Todd.

'I'm in.'

17

IF PERTH WAS JUNK MAIL, then Sydney was a postcard. The white slices of the Opera House roof curled into the blue sky. Ferries sailed off into smooth water. Towering ships arrived into port, almost eclipsing the Harbour Bridge. The sun was gentle with you and made sure you could take a perfect photo. Streets wound around each other, not sure what they wanted to do with themselves. Cobblestones rippled down laneways below sandstone walls. Every colour was richer, from the green of the trees to the red of the post boxes.

Shit coffee though.

The first show at the Opera House with Todd was incredible. The second was a dream. By the third day, work was work. The production staff knew my name now and Todd had stopped exclaiming my brilliance after each show.

It was Saturday and we couldn't get access to the stage yet because *Puppetry of the Penis* was doing a one-night-only performance of their world-famous dick tricks. I had a seat in the staff cafeteria, adding up all my earnings for the week on a notepad. The window in front of me displayed the Northern Beaches, shores dotted with houses only millionaires could wrangle mortgages for.

Todd texted me to come hang out in his green room. Calculating my net worth had only taken a few seconds so it was a fair alternative to boredom. When I arrived he was sipping whisky from a swanky tumbler. He tilted the bottle towards me as an offer.

'Sure,' I said. I'd built up enough currency with my previous performances to risk having at least one sloppy set.

'The Puppetry guys might be coming to visit too,' he said. One of the pigeons in a cage next to him cooed. It must have been into that kind of thing. 'Have you ever seen that show?'

'I haven't,' I said.

'Funniest show.' His whisky swished in its glass as he emphasised his sentiment. 'You think it would be just for older women and bachelorette parties. What do you call those here? You have a weird name for it?'

'Hens night.'

'Hens night!' He half stood. 'Hens night, yes. But the show is so funny. So, so funny. They get their dicks and—'

Before the pigeon could coo again, there was a knock at the door. I answered it to save Todd from an impromptu sobriety test.

'Hey, hey!' A pair of legs ten times my total height stepped into the room wearing a silky blue cape and underwear. That was it.

'What up!?' came from the next entrant, a much shorter man, wearing the same.

A woman followed behind in normal clothes, excited to see Todd and, more so, the pigeons.

The first guy embraced Todd and then turned to me. ‘Hey, I’m Rich. This is Barry, the other puppeteer. And this is my wife Olivia. She’s not in the show.’ He smiled.

‘I would never assume,’ I said, shaking everyone’s hands despite knowing where they’d been.

‘Oh my god, Todd what’s happening?’ Barry said, beaming. ‘We haven’t seen you since Vegas!’

‘No!’ Todd let the word stretch out longer than one of Rich’s legs.

‘Yes!’

‘That long?’

‘Three years.’

‘We all need to get naked to celebrate!’ the whisky said for him. We chuckled enough to make sure he knew where we stood on that suggestion. At least where I stood. I didn’t know any dick tricks, other than the one that might get someone pregnant.

‘How cute are these pigeons?’ Oliva said. ‘Do they have names?’

‘This one is Captain Poopy and the other two are Lou and Reed,’ Todd said.

‘Amazing,’ she replied.

‘Drinks! Grab some drinks! I have whisky and there are beers in the fridge.’ Todd got the others what they asked for, not before a playful argument with Rich, who only wanted water. Todd then stood on his chair and lifted his glass.

‘I just wanted to bring you all here to celebrate some amazing news!’ He was in full performer mode despite a slight wobble. I put my glass down just in case I had to catch my source of income.

'I just got a call today from my agent telling me I got a pilot on Comedy Central!' Todd bellowed.

The four of us cheered, whistled and clapped as he took a bow, spilling half his whisky onto the carpet.

'That's so good, dude!' I said, helping him down from the chair.

'When do you film?' Rich asked.

'We start pre-production in two weeks. If it works out I could have my own show by the end of the year.' He plopped onto his seat.

'That's amazing, babe,' said Barry, popping a kiss on his cheek.

Todd swayed forward in his chair, having to halt himself on the bench and prop himself up again. He reached for the bottle of whisky and poured about eighteen times the standard drink. Olivia gave me a look that said, 'Should he be doing this?' I gave her one back that said. 'Don't look at me.' Her next look said something else but I wasn't fluent enough in disapproving expressions to understand it.

***

Most of the crowd was laughing. Just not at the intended moment. Todd had so far dropped a bowling ball on his foot, lost a spectator's card, spilled water from a fishbowl onto the front row and dropped a multi-coloured hanky from his sleeve without noticing. The others and I had gathered in the wing on the side of stage to see if this helicopter could land without its rear propeller.

Todd was about thirty minutes into the first act, where he was beginning a trick called The Shell Game. It used three walnut shells, a green pea and a borrowed fifty dollar note from a man in the crowd who was asked to sign his name on it. Todd would move the pea around under the shells and ask the participant each night to guess where it was. A camera projected the effect onto a huge screen behind him so everyone could follow, making it all the more impressive when the pea appeared in an impossible place. Todd fumbled the pea before even starting, giving me and the Puppetry crew another layer of tension to the whole performance.

As intended, the crowd were staring up at the screen so there were only a few bewildered gasps from the audience when Captain Poopy shimmied his way out of Todd's briefcase and onto centre stage. Olive nudged Rich, pointing out the avian Houdini. Rich gaped at me, slapping his hands to his temples. I was already biting down on my bottom lip, glancing back and forth between Todd and the pigeon.

'What you gotta do is keep your ass on the pea… your eye on the pea. Not your ass.' Todd chuckled at his own gaff. 'That would be a different show.'

He placed a shell over the pea and swapped the other two around a few times. 'It's all about misdirection. You think you should be looking in one place but you really have to keep an eye on where I don't want you to look.'

I clicked my tongue at Captain Poopy to beckon him over. Approaching the bird would break the threshold of Todd's ability to hold a crowd's focus. Jack Daniels wasn't helping him either.

'Okay, here we go. Who did I borrow the money from again? David?'

'Steven.' Said the participant.

'Close enough. So Steven, which shell is the pea under?'

'The left one.'

'Willing to bet fifty bucks on it?'

'Not really.'

The audience liked Steven's sense enough to give him a giggle and applause.

'Then you shouldn't have handed me the money, Steven! Here we go. Fifty on the left shell.'

Todd lifted up the left shell, showing it empty. The middle shell was the same. The pea was under the right shell. Gasp. 'I guess this is mine now.' Todd shoved the note into his pocket, leaving his hand in there a second too long if you knew what to look for.

The Opera House roof swallowed up a fair swath of the chuckles but we'd learned the acoustics well enough by now to gauge a crowd. I edged as far forward towards the stage as I could without being seen by the spectators. Crouching down, I cupped my hands towards the pigeon to make it think I had seed or bird drugs in it.

'I'll give you two more chances to win your money back, Steve.'

Todd repeated the process of swapping the shells around. Steven guessed wrong again, as the participants always did. Captain Poopy had waddled further towards me but stopped about a metre away to pick at some fluro tape on the stage.

'Here we go, Steve. Can I call you Steve?' Todd didn't wait for a reply. 'Thanks. Okay, so I'm going to do this very slowly. I'm placing the pea right here. Is that fair Steve?'

'Sure.'

'You don't sound convinced but I'll take your word for it. I'm only going to use one shell now. I'll place it over the pea. Fair?'

'Yes.'

'I'm now going to place this shot glass over the shell so I can't get to that either. Okay?'

'Yep.'

'And I'll get rid of these two shells altogether.' Todd plucked up the shells from the table and placed them in his pocket.

'Now Steve, don't screw this up. You already owe me another fifty.'

Everyone laughed. Captain Poopy flapped with unease. Rich, Olivia and Barry were gritting their teeth. They knew, as I did, that a bird flying around the auditorium would ruin the second half of the show and be a nightmare to retrieve. It was on me to get the timing right.

'So, to get you out of debt Steve, where is the pea?'

'Under the shell.'

'Steve, Steve, Steve.' Todd shook his head. He lifted the glass and the shell to show it empty.

'You lost a lot of money tonight, Steve. Is that your wife next to you? I hope she likes you for your personality. I'll tell you what, I'm going to give you a consolation prize for being such a good sport. How about a nice, delicious unopened walnut?'

Todd brought out a walnut from his pocket. He turned it over in front of the camera to show it was intact. My foot was poised behind me, ready to spring me forward. The capture had to happen a split second before the applause scared the Captain into the lighting rig.

'In fact, let me open it for you.' Todd pulled out a nutcracker from his other pocket and snapped the shell open to reveal Steven's signed fifty-dollar note.

I pounced forward, slapped my hands over the pigeon's wings and withdrew back to cover before the applause reached its peak. The Puppetry gang were in silent hysterics next to me. My smile was prouder than it had been in ages.

When the show was over, I couldn't wait to tell Tash all about it. Western Australia was three hours behind so she'd be up. I called to no response. She had been sleeping a lot, maybe that was it. By the afternoon the next day my call was unreturned and my messages unread. The high from the show's shenanigans was soon replaced by dread. For the second time in my life, I wanted to get back to Perth.

18

IT WAS OVER FOUR WEEKS before I dumped my suitcase back down on Jin's unvacuumed floor. I had done a run of gigs in Melbourne, Brisbane and Adelaide in that time: just at clubs and bars, but enough to keep my rent paid. Not enough to pay Jin back yet. He didn't show any hint of caring. When I arrived he was packing his sneaker collection into moving boxes. A-List had already lined up work for him in commercial radio in Melbourne. He was to be the new host of the Fox FM graveyard shift. That would be easy enough for Jin as he already kept those hours, but he'd have to experience them sober now.

'Let's get smashed tonight,' he said, instead of hello.

'I don't know, man.' I eased down onto his bed and turned his TV on to flick around the channels. There were reruns of *Whose Line Is It Anyway*. Wayne Brady and Robin Williams were flailing strips of shaggy carpet around for the prop challenge. Robin used them as pom-poms and ad-libbed a cheerleader chant. A mix of sadness and awe swam around my stomach seeing him. It had been years since he passed away but his comedy energy still pulsed on. He embodied the idea of delivery over material. Give that man a slice of shaggy carpet and he could still out-funny the well-honed material of most comedians.

'Come on. It's my last week in Perth, bro!' said Jin.

'I guess. That's pretty fast, hey. I thought you'd at least start next month.'

'A-List doesn't mess around, bro.'

'That's great.' I might have sounded unenthused but I was just distracted by Wayne and Robin who were now wearing the carpet pieces on their heads.

'How's your missus?' Jin asked.

I switched the TV off and made for the door. Tash had been replying to my messages but with no consistency. I would get, 'Hey, sorry I missed your call. I've been pretty out of it', or the unkept promise of, 'I'll call you later'. Perhaps she had found support in her friend Krystal or the other guy and she didn't need me anymore. Each of the twenty times I called I let it ring all the way out to voicemail but would never leave one. That would just be desperate.

'She's good but she's not my missus.' I leaned against the doorway, ready to leave again.

'Why you back in Perth then?'

'You know I have a gig,' I said.

'You flew over for one gig?'

Air left my nose in a huff and I left his bedroom. His fridge had a whole bunch of nothing-with-sustenance in it.

'I don't feel up for going out tonight,' I called out.

***

Five beers in, I was yelling at Jin over the cover band at Rosie O'Grady's. He was either nodding at what I was saying or his head had filled up with so many vodka sodas it was swishing back and forth. The bar was full of other patrons shouting over the band's rendition of Amy Winehouse's 'Valerie'. Two women in tight black dresses were dancing in front of the stage, trying not to splash red wine on the floor, with minimal success.

'So I think she likes me,' my mouth was about a cigarette's width from Jin's ear. 'I just figure she's pretty confused right now. You know? I mean we were not hooking up. Just hanging out like friends but we did hook up once so it's still possible, right? She might just be comfus… com… confused.'

Jin kept nodding but he was now watching the women attempt to twirl under each other's arms, their feet spreading the wine puddles around the lino flooring.

'Yeah, I mean she's cute but I dunno,' I said. 'I dunno if I want to spend the rest of my life with her, you know? I like her. Like she's cute. Thanks for letting me stay at yours, man. You're a good friend.' My bottle of Coopers clinked into his glass to cheers our friendship. Jin put the glass to his lips out of reflex but it had been empty for a while.

'You should message her now,' he said. 'Tell her you want to see her.'

'I'm drunk.'

'You're not that drunk, bro.' Jin came clean off his chair and landed on his muscular glutes. I bent down to help him up. He was too heavy for me so I just sat next to him to make it look like we were chilling.

'Okay,' I said. 'I'll just tell her I'm thinking about her.'

'Great idea, man.'

Even autocorrect didn't attempt to fix the typos in my message to Tash. After two minutes in real time but four hours in drunk time, the message still hadn't been read by her.

'I'll just call her,' I said.

'Call her, bro! Tell her you want to have her baby… have your baby. Whatever.'

The call didn't even ring. Her phone must have been off.

'I'm… I'm just going to go see her.'

'Bro, that's a great idea.' Jin lay flat on the floor. The bouncer approached us and said it was time to move on. There were now multiple identical bouncers standing next to each other in my vision. I didn't argue with any of them.

Out front, Jin said he would walk home. 'Go get her, bro.' He stumbled off in the wrong direction.

There was a cab on James Street right outside the pub. It was easier to wave it down than fumbling around with my phone for an Uber. The driver flicked a nod at me and I opened the front passenger door, using it to steady myself so I could lift a leg without falling backwards. I'd been grounded enough tonight.

'Where to?' the driver asked, once I achieved the feat of entering the taxi.

'Kings Crescent, Mt Lawley,' I slurred.

'You mean Queens Crescent?'

'Yes! That one.'

'What number?' he asked.

'Any number.'

The driver might have looked confused but my focus was on not throwing up.

***

It only took twelve hours in drunk time for me to find the house. It had a white ute parked on the grass in the front yard and a barbecue outside the door. I remembered the barbecue because I'd accidentally put my hand on it while I was waiting for Tash to open the door all those months ago. I had to hide a blackened palm from her until I could get to the bathroom to wash it. Good times.

To sober up, I slapped myself a few times in the face and jumped on the spot. It either didn't work or it worked a treat but made me dizzy from the impact.

The doorbell chimed at my press. Not much was visible under the faint outdoor lamp above it. I pressed again just in case. Three times was the right amount. Before getting a chance to press it again, the door flung open.

'Who are you?' A guy about six-foot-lots squinted down at me from his genetic gift of height.

'H-hi, um.' I squeaked more than spoke. 'Is, er, is Tash in?'

'She moved out.' He began to close the door.

'Wait, where?'

'I don't know, man. Give her a call.' Before the door closed, my foot blocked it.

'Hey!' he said, kicking at my shoe. His runners were smattered with dirt and grass around the edges.

'She's not answering my calls, dude. I really need to…'

He was wearing shorts. They were blue with a crest of a falcon on the seam. Football shorts.

'Wait, are you…' It was dumb but my mouth said it before my brain had a chance to get involved. 'Are you the other dad?'

He stopped kicking. The door banged all the way open and he marched at me, his chin down and chest out. I stumbled back, keeping my distance.

'I'm not the fucking dad, okay!?' he said.

'Dude, I think you might be.'

'Who the fuck are you?' He shoved me backwards, acquainting my arse with the concrete path. My brain did a three-sixty inside my skull. Rage shot down my veins as if my cavemen ancestors had woken up inside me.

'Hey, fuck you!' I said, exercising my well-trained comedy wit.

'Fucking Tash.' The footballer shook his head. From inside the house, another voice called out.

'What's going on?' it said.

'Nothing,' the footballer yelled, turning towards the door.

I staggered off the ground and sprang forward, jumping on his back. There was no plan after that. I just hung on in anger while he flailed around trying to buck me off. He turned his back to the doorframe and heaved backwards to slam me into it. Still, my beta-male pride kept me gripping around his boulder shoulders. His elbow found its way into my liver and my arms released. Pain hit my abdomen. The footballer grabbed me by the collar of my t-shirt and dragged me towards the street.

It was at this time that I accepted I had made a mistake.

He dropped me onto the footpath and kicked me in the ribs.

'Fuck off.' He went back to the house.

Besides his tall stature, wide frame, muscular arms, chiselled jaw, thick footballer thighs, dark features and exceptional strength, I didn't know what Tash ever saw in him.

19

'SORRY I MISSED YOU last night. I've been moving house,' Tash wrote. 'Are you still in Perth?'

It was now my turn to delay a response. I was draped over Jin's couch, dabbing a wet t-shirt full of ice on my ribs. It was one of Jin's v-necks. Damaging it to the point he couldn't wear it anymore would be doing him a favour. It was mid-afternoon and the apartment was quiet. My attempt to fight a semi-professional athlete still gave me a rush of embarrassment. The headache didn't help either. I found my notepad in the outer part of my suitcase and wrote joke ideas.

- The word 'hangover' must be an abbreviation for 'hang-on-I-can't-do-anything-until-this-pain-is-over'.
- Best part of being short is people don't expect you to win fights.

It took me twenty-five minutes to come up with them and I hated them both.

Jin stepped out of his room dressed in sweatpants and a tank top. He looked like he'd been sober since birth. His hair was somehow tidy too, with his part showing in between shiny gelled slabs. There was enough product on that man's head to keep every strand in position for a decade.

'I'm off to the gym, bro,' he said. 'Want to come?'

'No thanks. I got a work-out last night.'

'Nice.' Jin went to the cupboard, pulled down the five-kilo container of Gold Standard protein powder and opened it before he registered my cryptic response. 'Wait, what?'

'I got into a fight.' I peeled the makeshift icepack off my shirt and jiggled it to show him.

'Bro!'

'It's okay. I think I won.' My voice was strained. 'I only bruised most of my body and he probably has a really sore toe from kicking me.'

'What the fuck? What happened?'

I recounted the events. There were moments in the retelling when I wanted to laugh. It was as if my actions the previous night had nothing to do with me but were just the ill-conceived capers of Drunk Ben. The problem was that Drunk Ben's mistakes ended up hurting Sober Ben's body. And ego.

As I spoke, Jin kept clenching his jaw and squeezing his fists.

'Let's go back!' he said. 'I'll come with you.'

'Let's one hundred percent definitely not do that.'

'I wanna bash this dog.' Jin pounded the benchtop. A puff of protein powder shot up from the container.

'Yeah and make sure that both potential fathers are injured before the baby is born. Great idea.'

Jin's fists rested on his hips and he shook his head. 'So she hooked up with you and then her housemate. Fuck, bro.'

'Shut up, man. You've stuck your dick in half the city.'

'Yeah but…'

'But what? But what, huh!?' The shirt of ice crunched in my hand.

'Calm down, bro. I was just saying.'

'Don't be a dick, okay,' I said.

Jin let the tension sit for a moment. 'Who do you reckon was better in bed, you or him?'

A laugh burst from my lips. My chest stung but it was worth it.

'You're an idiot.' I chuckled at him. He was alright. It was a sweet, yet physically painful reminder of why we became friends in the first place. When you do comedy long enough, you see so many jokes coming that you're less affected by them. So if you could make a comedian laugh, they'd cherish you. Lending them money helped too.

Jin scooped protein out from the container and lumped it into a shaker. He paused and exhaled. The air between us went still. The mood had flattened back down to sombre and we didn't say anything while Jin packed his backpack and opened the front door. Before stepping out he turned back.

'Do you want this kid, man?' he asked.

'If it's mine, of course,' I said without pausing to think.

'Yeah, but do you want it to be yours?'

I place the ice onto my forehead to slow my thoughts. They were interrupted anyway by the slight sound of my teeth grinding.

'It changes every day.'

***

Tash accepted my hug for only half a moment and patted my arm as if I were a distant relative she was obliged to greet. She sat further from me than she would have a few weeks ago. She had to ease her way onto the wooden bench by supporting herself on the brick wall behind it with one hand. Her belly had risen far faster than I would have guessed it could. It curved out from her body in the opening of her faux fur jacket. The baby bump called for my hand to rub it and say hello to the growing human inside. I resisted for now. There was still a human outside to attend to.

'What vegetable is it now?' I asked.

'Twenty-four weeks is corn,' she said.

'Corn? Has it gone backwards?'

'An ear of corn, not a kernel.'

'That makes more sense.' I cracked my knuckles and then placed my hands in three different spots before cupping them around my knee. My short wooden seat positioned me at a right angle to Tash, helping me avoid showing her the entirety of whatever my face was portraying. There was a car tyre mounted to the cafe courtyard wall. It was filled with small pot plants and knick-knacks. We were at Toastface Grillah, a cafe named after a rapper from the Wu-Tang Clan. Ghostface Killah himself even visited once when he was on tour a few years back, causing a mild stir on social media amongst Australian fans of nineties rap. It was surreal to see hip-hop emerge from a niche music genre into inspiration for a gritty urban cafe in an otherwise corporate city. Plus, I liked the funny name.

'Can I get you anything?' I asked.

'I'm not hungry,' she said and bit at her thumbnail.

'I'm going to get a grilled cheese. This place is cool, huh?'

'It's very Melbourne,' she said.

'The best stuff is always down laneways.' I made a knowing shrug.

I went inside to order the Danny Zuccho: cheese and zucchini. The classic three-cheese was better but I want to keep up my support for creative naming. The guy behind the counter told me he would bring it out.

Back outside, Tash was chewing her way through her other nails. Her skin looked fairer than ever. When I returned to my seat she spoke like the words had been ready to burst out since I had left for Sydney.

'Okay so I finally spoke to my doctor about getting a paternity test before the baby is born but it's risky,' she said. 'I know you want to find out sooner but I can't put the baby in danger. I couldn't live with myself if anything happened to …'

'Hey, it's okay. I understand. I would never make you risk the health of the baby. Or yours for that matter,' I said. 'I also figured that was how you felt since you never brought it up.'

Tash's whole body deflated with relief. 'Okay good. Thank you. I would be so scared to get it.'

'I would never put that kind of pressure on you. We can get the regular test when the kid is born.'

'I'm worried about that one too.' She stopped chewing her nails.

'That one's safe,' I said. 'It only uses—'

She cut me off. 'No, I mean I'm kind of worried about what the result will be.'

My teeth were grinding in my jaw again as I waited for her to explain.

'It's still so confusing,' she said, rubbing her forearm with the pads of her fingers. 'You've been so sweet to me.'

It wasn't much of an explanation so I dared to push for one. 'But you're still into the other guy?'

Before Tash could process the question, the cheese and zucchini sandwich arrived. It smelled of toasted bread and melted heaven. Before I took a bite, Tash postured up a fraction. The steam coming from it was distracting her.

'Here,' I said, offering it with an extended arm.

'I'm fine.' Her voice squeaked before the words came out.

'No, really. Eat.'

She didn't protest a second time. Her fingertips clasped it and she took a huge bite out of the corner. She didn't appear to flinch from the visible heat.

'I'll buy you another one,' she said. 'I'm not a toastie thief.'

'I wasn't going to call the cops, don't worry,' I said.

Tash took another bite, either out of hunger or to avoid answering my last question. The answer would have sucked anyway.

'I should probably tell you,' I began, deciding the toastie had bought me enough goodwill, 'I went past your place the other day and met the footballer.'

Tash looked like she had just noticed the toasted sandwich was three thousand degrees. I think she said, 'You what?' but it was muffled by bread and tasty cheese padding her mouth.

'I'm sorry,' I said. 'I was drunk and I really wanted to see you.'

'That is so…' Tash swallowed and then bit down on her bottom lip. There were other people in the courtyard near enough to keep her anger within polite parameters. She put the toasted sandwich down which indicated the intensity of her feelings.

'I'm sorry, okay,' I said. 'I just didn't know what was going on with us. I know I've been travelling and that's made it difficult to gauge where we're at.'

'Jesus,' she whispered in a way that somehow felt loud. 'What did you say to him?'

'We, um… we had a good conversation,' I said, with all the acting power a comedian could muster. 'And he seems pretty confident the kid isn't his.'

She shook her head. 'You mean he pretended like he even remembered that night. Fuck, I can't believe you actually went to my place. Fucking hell.' My knee was bouncing up and down while her emotions peaked. I had another dozen apologies ready to unload to keep her from swearing at me further.

Instead, Tash picked up the sandwich and resumed eating. A sign of peace. A long string of cheese formed between her teeth and the toastie. She tipped her head up to feed it in. Like an angel would.

'Can you really be angry with a string of cheese falling out of your mouth?' I asked.

'I can multitask,' she said, still chewing.

'Look, he might not want to get involved but I want to know that you and the baby are doing well. It's important to me.'

'Is that why you went to Sydney?' she asked.

'Hey, that's not fair! I still have to work.'

Tash coughed on the last mouthful. 'You're right.' She nodded with a solemn face. 'That was unfair.' She wiped her hands and mouth on a napkin before moving in and putting her hand on my cheek.

'Ben, you really are so sweet. I'm so lucky you even care. But it's… it's so hard to navigate all these feelings,' she said, leaning back now and folding her arms. 'But I still can't believe you spoke to T… I won't say his name. Do you know his name?' I shook my head. 'I can't believe you spoke to him. It's kind of weird actually.'

'Well it's done now.' I shrugged.

'Hmm. Well, I'll still get you a toastie because I'd feel guilty otherwise.' She reached for her purse. 'And thank you for feeding me. You know how I feel about gifts.'

'I do know how you feel about gifts.' I tipped my head forward to emphasise this knowledge.

'When do you head back to Melbourne?' she asked.

'I leave on Sunday. But hey, listen. Please send updates about the baby. I want to know all the vegetables. Is that okay?'

Tash had shuffled forward on the bench and placed her hand on the table in preparation to steady herself up. I was about to help but got caught admiring the grace she was still able to maintain with a corn-sized-bulge.

'Fine,' she said, 'but only because you gave me the toastie.' She stood up, leaned over and gave me a short kiss on the forehead. It did smell like a good toastie.

20

'WHAT DO YOU MEAN quitting?'

'As in not doing it anymore. You know, the standard definition of the word.'

'Libby, come on. You'll get back into it eventually.'

'I don't think so.' She stepped towards the counter at the souvlaki bar. 'I'll have a slice of the vegetarian, please.' Her finger pointed towards the pizza slices stacked on top of each other in the glass display.

'Two-fiddy,' said Eddie, his white hair thinner on his eyebrows than the top of his head. He'd been working the midnight shift here long before I ever needed post-show carbs. He always wore the same powdery apron and refused to raise the price of the pizza. Reliability is an underrated attribute. Comfort food was just as much about the person serving it as it was the amount of grease it held.

Libby and I stood outside, each with a floppy slice in our hands, watching people buzzing up and down Brunswick Street. The neon lights of the cafes and bars gave the Victorian era shopfronts a cool glow and a sense of energy in these late hours.

'But why?' I asked. 'Surely when things settle down with work you'll come back.'

'I'm tired, Ben. I'm tired of quiet crowds and shit gigs. It used to be okay when things with work and Dane were under control. His support really allowed me to do comedy. But I can't have a rough day and then come do a rough gig.'

A tingle formed in the corner of my eye and a small lump crawled into my throat.

'So that was your last gig then?'

'Yep.'

'At Dirty Secrets? You could have at least gone out with a bang.'

'I didn't start with one.' She shrugged. 'Why change it up now?'

We ate our slices, taking in the streams of cool kids gliding in and out of bars and stumbling from late-night cafes while holding kebabs dripping garlic sauce onto the pavement. Most people were in skinny jeans and vintage coats, either tan or black. The north side of the Yarra in Melbourne had always retained its bohemian fashion sense but had added some chic over the years to keep up with the demand for Instagram-worthy selfies.

'Well it's going to suck without you,' I said, the crust of the pizza making my cheek bulge.

'Thanks.' She chewed.

'Is Dane doing okay at the moment?'

'He'll be fine. He's back on antidepressants.'

'Damn,' I said.

'Yeah.'

'I'm here for you, mate.' I nudged my elbow onto her upper arm in place of an oily hand.

'Thanks mate.' She nodded. 'It'll all be fine.'

I knew it would but she appeared to be saying it to herself.

'Hey remember that gig we did at Falls Festival?' I said.

'Oh my god! That was so bad.' She chuckled. 'In that flimsy tent near the main stage? Literally the worst possible place to do a comedy show.'

'When *was* that?' I mused.

'Jeez, ages ago. I think we were both only a year in?' she said.

'Remember that dude in the crowd who had a baby carrier on his chest? And he had a bottle for the kid in one hand.'

'And a beer in the other! That was so messed up.' A happy Libby was a comfort I'd missed.

'Reckon that was your worst gig?' I asked.

'No. Watching you at the Exford was the worst one.'

'Of course. I'm honoured to make the top of your list.'

'It's quite an honour,' she agreed.

After wiping the oil from my fingers onto the back of my jeans, I checked an email that had just turned up.

'Holy shit,' I said, opening the notification.

'What is it?' she leaned over to see my screen.

The subject line read: 'I got the Comedy Central show!'

The email flashed open.

Buddy! I got the series! I'm looking for writers and you'd be so good. You want a job in LA?

'Holy shit,' Libby said, reading along.

We start in January and go for twelve weeks. Let me know? Would you be willing to move out here? Have to finalise writers by the end of the month.

Stay Magical.

Todd Power.

He had a black logo underneath his name with the initials T.P. with a bolt of lightning behind them.

'Fuck.' I squeezed my cheeks forward until my lips squished out like a fish. A very surprised fish.

'Congratulations!' Libby's excitement flew past my sunken shoulders.

'I can't go.' The phone sagged down into my pocket.

'What? Why?' she asked.

'Tash is due in January.'

Libby balled up the paper bag that had held her pizza, threw it two metres towards the bin and scored.

'Ben, listen to me. If you're the dad, this will give you income to support the kid. And if you're not the dad, fuck, go chase the career you always wanted.'

'Hmm.' The wind was cold now and wanted to send me home.

'Hey,' Libby cupped my face with both hands and pointed it towards her own. 'I'm never going to catch a break like this. Take it while you can.'

I nodded. It was enough to end the conversation with Libby but it continued on in my head.

'What are you thinking?' she asked.

'I think I want another slice of pizza.'

***

The setting sun frowned at me through the window, since I had ignored its pleas to do something, anything, with my day. I drafted a message to Tash but deleted it. Back to punching pillows. The deadline to make a decision about America was just outside the door, ready to pounce in and strangle me. My ability to think things through had been lost, along with any motivation to ever get out of bed. The sun could do what it wanted, I wasn't budging.

Even when I managed to go to the toilet, my knees felt weak and I had to lie down right after. The sheets hadn't been changed in centuries. My room was thick with the smell of stale sweat and my dread of the months to come. When my hunger was fed up with being ignored, the fridge got a reluctant visit. There was nothing in there I wanted to eat. By the third visit I was just seeing if my standards had dropped enough to stomach the last slice of swiss cheese on its own. They had. It was dry and stale so the best bits were the holes.

The last few weeks of messages from Natasha Peters scrolled under my fingers. The latest ultrasound was in 3D. A wax-like child had its big toe in its mouth. Its hand was resting against its face like it was bored of waiting. Other photos showed Tash in front of her childhood bedroom mirror, displaying her baby bump. Every image gave me a zap of adrenaline. The reality of fatherhood was growing faster each passing day. I wasn't sure what fruit or vegetable we were up to but I sensed watermelon was close.

The cheese went unfinished. My stomach had no room with all the anxiety swishing around it. It was time to ask the question that could release me.

'Hey Tash. This is a bit personal again but I'm just trying to get the dates clear in my head. Do you mind telling me the exact day you slept with the other guy? Sorry to pry! It will just help me understand something.'

The message wasn't going to come off well no matter how many apologies I sugared it with. But the question had been sitting in the pit of my gut for months now. The opportunity to flee to Hollywood had only aggravated it.

When I pressed send my fingers were trembling, my jaw was grinding and my blood froze over. The three dots started jiggling under the message – Tash was typing. They disappeared. She changed her mind. They appeared again and disappeared once more. The taunting dots followed the principles of torture. You never knew when shock or relief would be coming.

* * *

The message came at 8:52 p.m. the next night. Jin was doing a twenty-minute support spot at The Comic's Lounge. He was confident with every reason to be. He held the mic with a flexed bicep and rested his other arm on the mic stand to give off that relaxed-while-working vibe.

'I think smoking weed is making me paranoid,' he said. 'The problem is, the only way I know how to cope with being paranoid is smoking weed.' He showed his teeth in a wide grin, just to give the joke time to get a reaction from all four hundred people packed into the showroom.

'This one time, I was at a music festival and the sniffer dogs came out. So I ate my whole bag of weed.' The audience made gasps and delighted moans. 'If you think that's dumb, you should have seen me trying to swallow a cigarette lighter to set my stomach on fire. I could be a walking bong. Everyone would want to hook up with me!'

It got laughs from most of the room. The punchline was too wordy but he committed to the act-out of smoke puffing from his mouth. Everyone was on board by the end. It even broke me out of my analysis and I could just enjoy a friend doing well.

When the message from Tash arrived, I had to cup my hand around the screen to avoid distracting people with the light. Jin was doing a fine job keeping them engaged anyway.

'I slept with him on May 3. Why did you need to know?' Tash said.

The inside of my lip stung between the bite of my teeth. My notebook in my pocket contained the page Zack and I had plotted the ultrasound on all those months ago. The scribbled graph now appeared like it had been written by a much younger person, still trying to master the use of a pen. The estimated date of conception was written in large, black numbers. I chomped my lip again.

'That's all from me, I've been Jin Yeoh, have a sick night!' Jin left the stage and high-fived the MC, who announced the break. As soon as he did, I weaved passed the audience members heading to the bar and slipped under the curtain backstage.

Jin was talking to the headliner, Sean Scott, who was patting his shoulder.

'Bro!' Jin said when he saw me. 'You on tonight?'

'Just came to hang out,' I said.

'Fuck yeah.' He pulled me in for a half-hug. He thumped the back of my rib cage. It hurt in a friendship-affirming sort of way.

'And to say goodbye,' I said.

'Goodbye? Where you going?' He arched an eyebrow.

Sean and Jin awaited my response with concern on their faces. Behind the curtain, the crowd was chatting and clanging their glasses seemed to ease as I found my own clarity.

'LA'.

21

THE MESS OF BROKEN tools inside the wooden crate made it heavy and awkward to manoeuvre. The loose hammer heads and fragments of adjustable spanners gave a solitary clang as I dropped it down next to the box it had been sitting on. This is what I was looking for. Inside was a hessian bag that contained a dozen or so old tap handles. It took a tedious few minutes of paddling through the jumbled collection to find a matching pair. They both had 'C' on them, but this was the closest I was going to get to a budget replacement of the ones in my shower. I went back inside.

'Did you find them?' Dad asked, without looking up from the newspaper lying open on the kitchen table.

'I did. Am I good to take these?' I held the handles out, dropping one but then catching it against my chest before it fell too far. He didn't notice anyway.

'Do you know how to attach them?' he asked.

'I do.' I did not.

'I hope you get your bond back.' He raised his eyebrows but kept his eyes down. He was doing the crossword, in that old-school way with a pen and no cheating. He'd always write his first guesses in tiny letters in the corner of the boxes before committing to the full square. Some would just use a pencil. I peered over the table before sitting down to see the only word he had penned down in full size: 'LIMP'. I poised to make a 'there's a pill for that' joke but he spoke before I could showcase my Hollywood-grade wit.

'So the kid's not yours?' He kept writing tiny letters out.

'I don't think so. I mean, it's less likely to be me than the other guy.' I sat opposite him, placing the tap handles in front of me and toying with them with my thumb.

'You sure?' There was scepticism in his tone. The kind that he used when I said I couldn't find something in the house he knew was there.

'I am.' I wasn't.

Dad broke his focus from the crossword. Until now he hadn't looked straight at me. Since I had found out about his old habit, we hadn't connected like normal. At least I hoped it was an old habit; it was tough to know. There had been no tell-tale signs back when it was happening. As the money in Dad's savings had depleted, the facade of his life had never changed. Photos were still on the walls, he kept planting new ferns, even his choice in cuisine hadn't devolved. Any further. Dad had managed to contain a crisis and keep it from me, like I had with him. At least for a time.

'Look,' I said, 'if I'm the dad I should be earning some money. If I'm not, then I'm making the right move anyway.' They were Libby's words but they fit me enough. Logic and reason could outshine core values if you wanted them to.

'Hmm.' He rubbed his chin. His tone was more, 'I'm not convinced' than, 'Is that so?'. That's how I heard it. There was something else he wanted to say but I wouldn't prompt him to say it.

'Anyway, are you able to drive me to the airport next week?' I asked. 'That would be nice. Say goodbye for a few months.'

'I can do that.' He went back down to his paper. 'Dystopian.' He wrote in nine-across. It made me wonder if he had been looking at me or just in my direction while considering the all-important clues.

'I might be able to afford to get you a new car if Hollywood works out.' I said, inspecting my nails for excess confidence.

'That would be good.'

'What would you want? What's your dream car?'

'My dream car?' He gazed out the window. 'An electric car wouldn't hurt.'

'Great. I'll get you a golf cart.'

I struck the laugh I'd been digging for. When Dad smiled, even his crooked teeth couldn't diminish his charm. His laugh was breathy and wholesome. He'd scrunch his cheeks up revealing his fading dimples, one of which I had inherited, the other which Penny got.

'Hey.' I walked around to his side of the table. 'Give me a hug.'

He embraced me, dropping his pen without hesitation. His body had softened over the years but all the gardening had kept his hugs strong. I squeezed more to test his bones and show him the raw power I had gained from eating pure frozen peas.

'It's exciting,' he said. 'You might meet some celebrities like Rowan

Atkinson.'

'I'm pretty sure he still lives in England, Dad. But, hey, who knows?'

We finished our hug with light pats on each other's shoulders. He turned to a photo on the wall. One with my mother in it. He might have been wondering what she would have said about this whole situation. Her bright, cheeky smile in the picture suggested that it would have been witty and wise.

'You know, I'd like to be a grandfather one day,' he said. 'Have family around more.'

I bet he did, but there had been enough betting in this family for now.

The clock above the dining table made its tick known.

'By the way, is there anything you need my help with around here before I go?' I asked.

'There's always something.'

'Well you better think fast, I'm deep in packing boxes at home.'

'No, you head off home. I'll see you next week.'

I found my backpack at the back door, placed the tap handles inside, swung it around my shoulders and gave my father a casual salute.

'See you next week, Dad.'

'You will.' He rapped a knuckle on the table. 'You know what I just thought of?'

'What's that?'

Dad led me into his bedroom. The top drawer of his white dresser creaked open and he felt around for something. A red and green lump of cloth emerged.

'That's not…' I began.

'This,' he said, 'is your Robin costume from when you were five.' His dimples were as deep as they could be.

'How is this still in your top drawer?' My mouth hung open. When I was that age, Dad would dress up as Batman so that we could team up fighting crime in the form of cardboard cut-outs.

'Because, son,' Dad said. 'That's where I keep the important things.'

Our hug was longer this time. Dad told me he'd hold onto the costume for my kid to wear one day. I no longer wanted to consider how long away that was.

Before I left, Dad returned to his practical self. 'Let me know if you do more damage to the shower tap. I'll come help.'

'I will, Dad.'

He gave me another grin for the road.

As I plodded away from the house, Penny's white BMW pulled up to the curb. Her face was visible under the shine of the windshield, just enough to see her jut her chin out at me. I smiled and showed her my middle finger. That was my way of telling her I got a job, was going to be paid more than her, that she couldn't lord her support for Dad over me and that my commitment to a fickle career had finally paid off.

She gave me the finger back and smiled too. That was her way of telling me she didn't give a shit.

***

When I got home I threw the backpack onto the bed and tapped my laptop on. An email from Todd in my inbox confirmed my flight. I'd asked to get it next Thursday. At 4 p.m… from Perth.

22

THE HOSTEL IN NORTHBRIDGE looked like a Mexican villa. Its red arches frowned at me as I approached. I clunked my rolling suitcase up the steps. It had all my socks and the weight of my rash decisions in it.

At reception, a young guy wearing harem pants and a loose cotton shirt sat with his feet on the table watching anime on the computer screen. It was Dragon Ball Z, a kids' anime that was famous for stretching out a brief tense moment into multiple episodes, which, depending on your perspective, made it either riveting or excruciating to watch.

'Hey, I'm checking in,' I said. His lack of response put our scene into the excruciating category. 'Hello?'

'Check-in doesn't open until eleven.' He didn't even look up from the screen. It was 10:47 a.m. In Dragon Ball Z terms, it would take three hundred episodes for check-in to be open. The guy stared at the screen, chewing gum with his mouth open.

'Come on, man,' I said. 'It's pretty much eleven.'

'It's 10:45. The rooms won't be ready yet.'

'Can you check?'

The guy groaned as he hit the spacebar to pause the cartoon. He whipped the curser across the screen and clicked a few times, yanked open a drawer and plucked out a key. A stack of bedsheets and pillowcases sat on the shelf behind him. He took one of each and slapped them on the counter.

'Room three-zero-seven. I need your ID and credit card.'

He took my cards and I signed the form he passed over. He threw the form towards a pile of others but it caught the air and escaped to the floor. He bent down to pick it up and knocked the pile over. He swore in German. Or maybe it was just aggressive French.

'Um thanks for that, dude,' I said, collecting my cards.

'Hello, we're checking in.' A couple of sunburnt Brits stood behind me with two backpacks each, strapped to both their fronts and backs. The guy behind the counter tilted his head back and rolled his eyes. With my sheets under my arm, I hurried down the hallway. That Dragon Ball Z episode would never end.

At room 307 and I dumped the sheets onto one of the lower bunks. The other three beds in the room appeared to be claimed by wild animals. Half a dozen lumpy backpacks were strewn across the floor. The smell of compressed sweat made me wince. I opened a window but it only went up a few inches. It must have been a safety precaution to stop people jumping out when they remembered that this was the best accommodation they could afford. Sitting on the bed, I pulled the collar of my t-shirt up over my nose and opened a Facebook message to Tash.

'Hey, I'm in Perth for a couple of days for shows and stuff,' I lied, 'Can I come meet you somewhere?'

My eyes shut as I lowered to the pillow. The stink of the room kept my breath shallow. My heart made an occasional pang to remind me that LA could be a mistake. When I opened my eyes, four hours had passed. There hadn't been any sleep. It was more of an anxiety paralysis.

Tash had replied.

'Hey! You never said you were coming? Maybe you did and I missed it. Sorry. I can meet you tomorrow. Do you mind if we meet in Mandurah? It's about halfway between my parents' and Perth. I'm too tired to come all the way into the city and I don't want to make you come all the way out here to Bunbury.'

I breathed deep, despite the haze of mildew. One last meeting with Tash before I left.

'Of course. Just tell me when and where xx'. The message was sent before I realised I used two kisses. If I was here to tell her I was leaving, I needed to ease up on the excessive affection.

The door opened. A tall guy with arms drenched in tattoos stood next to a short blonde woman wearing peach short shorts. He held a plastic bottle filled with juice and I could smell the alcohol on his liver. The woman burped.

'Hey bru.' Tall man slurred at me. 'Bru, can you giv us a munute?'

The blonde girl giggled. Either at what he said or at something hilarious taking place inside her own head.

'Day drinking, huh? I'm pretty sure that's a pathway to citizenship,' I said but just for me.

I hopped off the bed, danced over the luggage on the floor and left them to add their exotic body odour to the room.

In town, the city was warm and content. The sky had a pink smile as the sun faded over the river. The buildings stood over me like older siblings, welcoming me back for the visit despite our intense history. The only sounds were the gentle hum of a car or the ticking of a green pedestrian light. Christmas decorations were already appearing in shopfronts. A steel angel hung on wires above an intersection, surrounded by plastic green wreaths on lampposts. I wondered how cold Los Angeles would get and if I would wear the jacket Tash bought me while over there. I'd spend most of my time in a writers' room anyway, tossing around jokes and eating giant American corn chips. Then I'd drive an SUV down to The Comedy Store for a quick set and crash a party in Beverly Hills. There. No guilt-laden jacket needed.

Perth let me stroll around until it was dark. No one in the city tried to kill me this time.

I guess we can all change.

***

Instead of making jokes about Perth, I should have been making fun of Mandurah. It's a beachside suburb about an hour away from the city and a decade behind it. Walking from the train station to the cafe Tash had picked, I counted three shopping trolleys in places they shouldn't be. One was on a roundabout, another was in the middle of the road and a third was hanging upside-down over a fence post. Either this was the trashiest part of the suburb or the most committed modern art installation I'd ever seen.

A strip of cafes ran opposite a park on the waterfront. The area was pretty and well-groomed. No trolleys here. A teenaged-looking woman passed me pushing a pram. She wore a crop top, showing her pierced belly button. Her eyes were tired as she focused on her phone screen, texting with one hand. I didn't run up to her and ask, 'Who got you pregnant?' but I had so many facts about contraception I wanted to share with him.

At the Hummingbird Waterside Cafe, Tash sat out front. Her hair was browner than the last time I saw her and tied up in a bun. Despite the sun being out, she was wearing a black hoodie and had her hands curled up under the sleeves. Her belly was hidden under the creases of her top. It could have contained any size vegetable.

Tash's face was fuller than I remembered and her cheeks were even rosier. It showed a dimple. She began to get up for me but I waved her back down. She held on to my hug for a while.

'Can I get you anything?' I asked.

'I'm fine, I just had a green tea. If I drink too much I'll pee all the way home.'

'That will help you find your way back here at least,' I said. Her lips curled up.

'It's warm, we could get ice-creams,' I said.

Tash's eyebrows shot up. 'Yes! I'll have an ice-cream.'

She had been sombre until that moment. It was as if too many obstacles built up around her in every direction until she had given up trying to cope with them. Now this knight in skinny black jeans had arrived and offered her a pathway to salvation through pasteurised milk products. That was me. I was the knight.

I clopped inside the cafe on my imaginary steed and returned with two cones of chocolate ice-cream. I passed her one like a royal chalice.

'Madam.' I bowed as she took it.

'Madam? Does this make you a jester?'

'I was going for a knight, but I'll take that.'

'I could make you a costume with a little bell on the hat,' she said, starting on the ice-cream. 'You could pull it off.'

'I'm still waiting for you to make me a wrap dress.'

It might have made her laugh if the cone wasn't being pushed into her mouth. I assumed it would have, for my own self-esteem.

'Before I forget…' My back pocket contained a thin brown package. It had been wrapped with precision. Every strip of tape was lined up with the edges and symmetrical on both sides. So in typical form, the journey inside my pocket had mangled it into a clump of creases.

'What's this?' Tash asked.

'I figured you never had a baby shower, so I got you a gift.'

'Ben! You didn't have to. Oh my god, this is so sweet. Thank you.' Tash caressed it with her free hand. She tore the package open on the table with one hand and an elbow while still holding the ice-cream. Very talented. Inside was white baby bib and with bold lettering across the front.

'Back in Bibness,' she said with a puff through her nose. 'Maybe you *are* the dad with bad jokes like this.'

'I learned from the best.' I shoved the ice-cream into my mouth.

Tash leaned back in her chair and pressed the bib to her chest. Her breath became short. A tear fell below her eye as her lips now curled downwards.

'Thank you.' Her wrist caught a tear.

I moved my chair around the table so it was close to her. Our hands held each others'. We didn't speak. The skin on her knuckle was wet from the tear. I gently passed my thumb over it until it dried. We just sat there until the earth began to revolve around the sun again and the ice-cream melted into their cones.

'I'm sorry,' I said.

'What for?'

'Just this whole situation.'

'I feel like I should be apologising to you,' she said. 'I let my feelings get in the way of doing what is right for the baby. And I pushed you away and then asked for your help. I'm really sorry. It must have been so confusing.'

'I'll tell you what. When you have the baby it can grow up and apologise to both of us,' I said.

'He.'

'What?'

'*He* can apologise to both of us.' She placed our hands on her belly.

A son. I could see us hanging out together already. Lego. Star Wars toys. I'm not sure what he would be playing with, but I might share. He'd want to learn basketball but I'd warn him of the mistake I had made growing up, thinking I would get tall enough to keep playing after turning twelve. My dad might have failed to explain how genes worked but I'd tell my boy every sport to avoid. It would be most of them, save for table tennis and Mario Kart.

'He's going to love ice-cream as much as his mum,' I whispered. This made her sob as her next works struggled out.

'And hopefully his dad.' Her hand squeezed mine.

I placed my cone on the table and let it drip onto a napkin. We watched it until she was calm again.

'Have you tried speaking to the other guy at all?' I asked.

'He still doesn't think it's his. He stopped responding to me,' she said.

'I didn't know that was an option.' I tried to bite the words back but they were gone. My comedy reflex had sprung before my brain had a chance to get involved.

'Fuck you.' Tash slapped my shoulder.

'I'm kidding.' It was a plea more than an explanation.

'It's not funny!' Her arms crossed.

'I'm sorry, I'm sorry.'

'You can't just joke your way out of this,' Tash spat.

'I'm sorry. Fuck, I don't know how else to deal with it sometimes.'

'How do you think I feel!?'

'I know, I know! It's much harder for you. I have no clue what it would be like to have something growing inside of you. I'm just so messed up about my involvement in this I can't think straight let alone imagine what you're going through.' My temples pulsed under my fingers. The ice-cream was still sticky on my skin. 'I'm talking in circles. I don't know what I'm saying.'

'Neither do I,' Tash said.

'What I'm saying… what I'm trying to say,' I sighed, 'is that if it's the other guy, I was hoping he'd be there for you and the kid. Because I… I have an opportunity in America that I'm leaving for, in a couple of days.'

Tash had put her cone down now too. The puddles of our melted ice-cream met in the centre of the table. They merged into one and dripped off the edge into oblivion.

'Okay,' she said.

'Okay?'

'Yeah, okay. Do what you want. I don't give a shit anymore. I told you when this started I could do it without you. I have my parents and friends now anyway. It looks like both the potential dads couldn't give a fuck about me or the kid. So just do what you want.'

'No, no, no. Hold on,' I said. 'I want to be able to do the test when I get back.'

'Maybe I don't want you to.'

'Tash, please.'

'I'll let you know when the kid's born. If you're around, you're around.' Tash got up. Her stomach appeared to be a mini planet now that she was standing. I fell out of its orbit as she began to walk away, one hand on the back of her hip and the other wiping her face.

'Tash don't go.' I stood up but she swore at me again, turning other people towards us. The teenage-mum was standing near the cafe entrance giving me a stare packed with judgement and warning. This could all escalate. I didn't want to be the guy harassing a pregnant woman in a public place. Or a private place. I was meant to be a knight, not a villain. Tash left me to back down. Terror hit me. *How can I be in the child's life if she doesn't want me there?*

The bib lay on the table, soaking up what was left of the ice-cream. I threw it in the nearest bin.

23

THE FASTEN SEATBELT SIGN was on. I took my designated middle seat and clipped in. Then I realised I might have to get up for the person coming through to take the window seat, so I grappled with the buckle again and released it. After four seconds, no one had come so I buckled up again just in case I forgot to put the belt back on and maybe get told off by the cabin crew. Now that was settled, every other decision in my life preoccupied me. I unbuckled to get my phone out and then buckled up again. I Googled the odds of withdrawal failure rates once more. My brain still hadn't caught up to the habit my fingers had developed. We hadn't been asked to put our phones on flight mode yet. I searched ultrasound statistics, just in case I'd missed anything the last six thousand times. There was nothing to find except discomfort and ads for erectile dysfunction pills. They only seemed to have pills that stopped erectile dysfunction. I needed one that would induce it.

There was a hum of American voices around me. They were in the standard accent, nothing exciting like Texan or Bostonian. Todd Power was originally from the Midwest but when you spoke to him he sounded as Hollywood as a soap opera. Either the people on this plane were raised in California or they had dropped their hometown accent for the fashionable one from movies too. My tongue felt too heavy to take on an American accent. I had the lazy 'r' sound set deep into my slack Australian jaw. I whispered the word 'burrrrgerrr' to myself a few times, trying to find mouth muscles I'd never used. It could take years to make it sound natural. Tash's expected delivery date was only a month away. My return flight was three months after that, long enough for a baby to learn how to babble in an Australian accent. If the Comedy Central show got renewed for more seasons I might be away for years, long enough for a baby to learn how to say, 'Where the fuck have you been?'

The seats next to me hadn't been filled yet. The God of Plane Seats was keeping them empty so I could turn my row into a bed during the flight, otherwise known as 'poor man's first class'. Perks of this class also included three times the pillows and a feeling that you'd won a minor lottery. My leg jittered. Every time someone walked along the rows checking their boarding pass and seat numbers, I'd direct telepathic insults at them. *Don't you fucking dare take these seats, old man. Keep walking, lady. You better take that toddler of yours all the way to the back of the plane, you motherfu—*

A young couple approached my row with their toddler.

'Do you mind taking the window seat?' The dad asked. I unbuckled again and moved over.

The couple both thanked me as they manoeuvred into their seats.

The kid had curly black hair that bounced as she hiccupped. A nappy popped out from her pink pyjama pants giving her a bulge befitting a

Kardashian. Her parents grappled with bags, backpacks, stuffed toys, bottles, books, an iPad and everything else from their house, tucking it all in the seat pockets and the gaps between us. The father sat next to me and took the toddler on his lap. She said she was hungry. Well, she said she was 'hungy' but we all knew what was up. The mother passed her a cracker to maximise the potential mess that could be made. The dad showed me his apologetic, sunken eyes as most of the crumbs landed on my lap.

'Sorry,' he said. The kid stood up on his legs and he had to support her attempt at balance.

'It's okay. I get hungy too.'

When the cabin doors closed, the toddler's cracker was gone from her hand and a layer of crumbs now covered, from what I could tell, the entire plane. A laugh broke through my discomfort and out through my nose. The kid was cute. Her rosy cheeks glowed under the low cabin lights. Her clumsy movements were hard not to adore. She settled into her father's lap in some inhuman pretzel shape, the hiccups still making her tiny body pop every so often. The engines started up. The pink-panted child began to cry. Her parents comforted her with rocking, pats and shushes. The row next to us put their headphones on like synchronised swimmers doing a flourish. The kid's baby teeth were on display through a strained yet delicate face. I turned to her.

'Hey hey, look.' I pulled my ears apart and poked my tongue out. She froze, bewildered. My tongue pulled back in at another press of my nose. She had never seen such magic. I pulled my ears again to pop my tongue out and pointed to my nose. Her dad got the game before she did and guided her soft-skinned fist to touch my nose. My tongue vanished once more. A fleeting giggle emerged. We repeated the game until she found my nose by herself. It lasted a couple of rounds before she tried other parts of my face. The effects varied. A touch on my chin got a fart sound. One on my forehead closed my eyes or reopened them. If she only touched one ear, my tongue would come out crooked. If only this kind of world-class entertainment worked on stage.

'What's her name?' I asked.

'Lily.' Her dad said.

'Wow. *My* name is Lily.' I'd won the whole family over now.

The announcement told us it was time to put our phones in flight mode, so I opened Facebook messenger. Tash hadn't been in touch. I wriggled in my seat a bit then realised I'd left my belt unbuckled. Of course. It clipped back in but the feeling of insecurity stayed. I inspected my calendar app and counted out how long it would be before a paternity test. Then a thought surfaced. I searched for paternity test laws in Australia. I heard Lily say she was hungy again. On a government website there was a link for paternity information. There was an FAQ. I wanted something like, 'How long can you wait before getting a paternity test so that you still have legal rights to see the child even though you weren't sure if it was yours so you took a comedy writing job for a magician in America?'. Turns out that question wasn't frequent enough.

As I was reading over the general information on the site, a message came in from Tash.

It only had three words.

My belt clicked again and I stood up in that awkward crouched way you have to in the row. The parents only offered me blank expressions, though their posture told me they weren't prepared to move for me until I said something. I stood up on my seat, stepped on the hand rest and leapt into the aisle.

'Sir, I'm going to have to ask you to take your seat.' The crew member in a deep red dress moved towards me. She used the phrasing of a professional that didn't want to appear bossy. No one needs to put 'I'm going to have to ask you' before a demand, it just softens the fact that you don't have a choice. She hadn't realised yet that I only had one choice.

I opened the overhead locker.

'Sir, take your seat.' Now she was serious.

'I need to get off this plane.' My blood ran at double speed. Her hands were held up at me. The murmurs around us had gone quiet and I could feel everyone's curiosity.

'I'll see if we can still open the cabin door.' She turned to another cabin crew member and asked them to check.

I tugged the strap of my backpack from the overhead locker. The pack slid off and hit me in the face. No magical effect happened this time.

'Sir, the cabin door is open if you want to…'

'Yes, thank you.' My heart was sending haymakers into my ribs. I hurried down the aisle, quizzical faces poking out at me. Off the plane I went, out the gate and back through security. They asked me some questions and accepted the answers. I jumped up the escalator steps two at a time and sprinted to the taxi rank. The cab driver up the front was leaning on the bonnet of his car, chatting to his co-worker but I cut in. He grimaced before turning on his professional face.

I could feel my pulse in every part of my body. Sweat covered my palms and there might have been a trail of it behind me. My voice cracked.

'I need to get to Bunbury Hospital.'

24

THE GLASS DOORS SLID OPEN and I ran into the smell of hand sanitiser. My arm felt light without a suitcase to drag but my legs still had to carry a chest full of adrenaline. I darted up to the hospital reception and got the attention of an older woman with thinning brown curls. She finished typing something before looking up at me through her half-moon glasses. My heavy breathing and frantic eyes didn't stir her.

'I'm trying to find Natasha Peters. She's giving birth right now.'

'Are you related?' she checked.

'Yes, I'm her… I'm the father.'

'Her father? You're quite young.'

'I'm the kid… the father of the kid!'

'Well you better get in there.'

'That's… yes, that's what I'm trying to do.' I squeezed my hands together to stop them from pulling the reception sign off and throwing it down the hall. The woman peered at a folder on the desk and slid a stupid finger down a stupid list of stupid names. From the outside, the hospital had appeared no bigger than a supermarket. At the pace her finger was going

I could have searched every room and returned before she was done.

'South Wing, one-one-four.' She said. I didn't wait for her to look back up at me.

'Wait! You need to wash your…'

The hallway took me to a set of signs pointing to each wing but a woman's muffled scream came from the right. I pivoted down the corridor and raced past open doors, following the sound to the last room. The door labelled '114' was closed but the yells were behind it and along with a voice saying, 'Okay, it's time to…'

I opened the door. Tash was on the bed, legs propped up and apart. Strands of her hair stuck to the sweat on her face as her lips curled in pain. She turned to see me step in.

'Ben!'

'Push! I need you to push now!' A doctor in green scrubs was standing at the end of the bed between Tash's stretched legs. There was a calm assertiveness when she spoke. Another woman, a nurse I guessed, was next to her in matching scrubs, holding Tash by her knee.

'Excuse me!' The nurse said to me.

'He can stay,' Tash said through her teeth. I rushed to her side as she let out a howl I'd never heard a human make. Her hand grabbed towards me. I gripped it hard. Her grasp was strong.

'You got this,' I said. 'You've so got this.'

The doctor put her gloved hands in position to catch something the size of a coconut. 'Here it comes,' she said.

'Tash you've got this, come on.' My voice cracked as tears welled in my eyes.

Tash let out a wail intense enough to expand the size of the room. Her body bent forward. Air sucked through her clenched teeth. The squeeze of her fingers cut off the blood in my hands. Every maternal ancestor could be felt in her grip. Vitality pulsed through her: wild and human and beautiful.

'You can do this!' I yelled. She pushed again, the muscles in her body were tense and strained. Her pained expression deepened while time paused to let her focus. It resumed as Tash gave way to an exasperated breath and flopped backwards on the pillow. A tiny body screamed into the world. The doctor held the baby up for us to see. His arms and legs stretched out into existence as the hospital lights met his pink skin with the glow of new life. Tash was panting, her grip around my hand now loose but still there. Her eyes glistened at her newborn son. Her work both done and just beginning.

A wet streak came down my cheek.

'Are you the father?' The doctor asked me as she snapped off her gloves. The sweet child held my warm gaze.

'I hope so.'

***

I sat beside an exhausted woman, her eyelids drooping with fatigue. The baby had been taken to the intensive care unit for monitoring about twenty minutes ago. The doctor said this was the procedure for premature births. If that kid only knew how much drama people had to deal with in life, he might have stayed in there a bit longer.

'When did they say we could visit?' Tash asked me through a slack jaw.

'The nurse said she'd come tell us,' I responded. 'He'll be okay.'

Tash winced. The air in the room was a mixture of musty odour and sanitiser. Heavy. Tash tried to shift her weight upwards to adjust her position on the pillow but gave up. It must have been even heavier for her. Tash found my eyes. Her hand reached towards mine and I helped them meet. My throat cleared itself in case more comforting words felt like coming out. They never did.

The nurse arrived, peeling off her gloves.

'Good news, he's doing fine. You can come visit when you're ready but we have to keep him in the incubator.'

Tash and I released breaths we didn't know we had been holding.

'I'll go,' I said, standing up.

'Ben.' Tash held on to my hand. 'I want to come.'

'I know, but you rest up. I'll be right back.'

She didn't have the energy to protest. The nurse took me down the hall and into where the baby lay sleeping in a clear plastic box. A tube ran under his nose, leading past wires stuck onto his chest. Machines on metal stands stood around him beeping and flashing lights and numbers. I placed a hand on the top of the incubator.

He was safe.

The nurse left me to imagine my life with him. First steps and first words. Thrown bowls of cereal. Awkward conversations during dinosaur movies. He'd learn to walk and dance and kick and joke. The most valuable of life skills. There was a Robin costume waiting for him too, and many crimes to deliver to justice with his dad. Whoever that may be.

On my way back down the hallway, a middle-aged couple was looking around at the room numbers. The man had a round face and only a few patches of hair above his ears and the woman had a slender nose much like Tash's. Their pace was frantic and their faces wore concern.

Instead of following them towards Tash's room, I turned off towards reception and left.

25

IN THE MORNING I called the lab from my dorm room bed and arranged a time to give my sample. If the backpackers around me could make baby-making noises all night, I could at least make paternity-checking ones. A confirmation email from the lab listed the requirements for the collection day: my passport, extra passport photos, a series of legal forms and a portion of my living human flesh. It was only going to be a few cells from my inner cheek but at this point, I was happy to submit my entire arm.

I read every line of each form about three times over. I had visions of a future courtroom where I explained to the wig-headed judge why I hadn't ticked the right box. 'You see, your honour, I just thought it was like the Facebook Terms and Conditions where no one reads it but agrees to it anyway.' Then the judge would throw the book at me, but in a literal way, smacking me in the face and causing the courtroom to point and jeer. Most of the form was just about not suing the lab if they got something wrong. The rest was about promising I wasn't lying about who I was. Lucky for me it didn't exclude having an identity crisis.

The bottom of the main identification form read: 'Identification and signature must be witnessed by a Justice of the Peace.'

All I could think about was the superhero movie *Justice League* with Superman, Batman, Wonder Woman and the fish guy.

After a slow, deliberate breath I adjusted myself on the pillow. Justice of the Peace was a foreign term to me. The internet revealed that they usually deal with affidavits, immigration forms, contracts and bail agreements. No wonder they didn't have their own movie yet. In this case they just needed to verify my identity. It now made sense that sending a DNA sample overseas for a prenatal test wouldn't be recognised in Australia; the courts couldn't trust people wouldn't falsify their documents. The price of deception would be less than child support if you wanted to be a dick.

An online directory gave me a list of local JPs. I called the first one: some guy named Leonard Albano. He had a trustworthy sounding name and scrolling down wasted time.

'Hello?' said the oldest sounding man in the entire world. He had a sharp Australian accent that shot through his nasal cavity like it was coming from a bird's beak.

'Ah, hi. My name is Ben, I have some forms that need to be witnessed by a Justice of the Peace.'

'Right. Yep. Come around.'

'Okay, er, what's your address?'

'Thirty Rrrffrrfd Road,' he said.

'Sorry, what was that?'

'Red-fern Ro-da.'

'Okay thanks very—'

He hung up. I found a USB drive in my bag and transferred the forms to it. There was no printer at the hostel but there was an Officeworks down the street. The woman at the printing station had a great big grin on her face until her eyes skimmed the heading of my forms.

'Here are your documents,' she said, making eye contact with everything but me.

'Thanks. I'll be a loving father,' I said and shot out the door before her disapproving frown caught up to me.

It took a train and a bus to get to number thirty Redfern Road. It was a strange house, the strangest part being that it was an empty block of land. The wind carried my swear words down the road. I called the JP again.

'No, no. THIRTEEN Rrddfrn Road,' he said. The rattling sound on the call was either the dodgy phone line or his false teeth.

'Okay. I'll be there in one minute.'

Redfern Road was one of those dumb roads where the change in suburb messed with the house numbers. I ran for ten minutes before number thirteen turned up. A white nursing home stood before me, a wheelchair ramp twisting up towards an automatic door to the foyer. At reception I was greeted by a middle-aged, stout man and the smell of talcum powder.

'I'm here to see Leonard.' I was still panting and the forms in my hand were distorted in my sweaty grip.

'No worries, sir. Just sign in for me thanks. He's in room 43,' he said, then pointed behind me. His arm was muscular. Perhaps human growth hormone helped with having to lift seniors out of bed. 'You want to head that way.'

Down the hall, I passed a living room where a dozen senior citizens watched *Better Homes and Gardens* on a widescreen TV. A piano stood in the corner, dusty and unloved. There was a temptation to nab a free mint from a bowl on the coffee table. Thrift had become a reflex but it was overridden by haste this time. Room 43 was close by and the door was open. An old man was napping in an armchair.

'Leonard?' I knocked on the doorframe with my pinkie knuckle.

'Who are you?' he asked, startled.

'I'm, ah, I'm Ben Thomas. I called you to witness some document signings.'

'Oh yes. Alright, what do we have here?'

Leonard left his armchair to sit at a small pine desk. This process appeared to take another nine months. He hunched forward and held onto the furniture to support himself. He poked through the documents I placed in front of him.

'Where do I sign?' he asked.

I pointed to the section for the Justice of the Peace. He scribbled a line that was indistinguishable from a cardiac arrest on an ECG. Leonard rummaged around his top drawer for a moment, pulled out an official-looking stamp and slammed it onto the document. He checked the passport photo attached and squinted up at me.

'Is that you, is it?'

'Yes,' I said.

'Alright.' He might have shrugged if his shoulders weren't so stiff.

He handed the paper back to me, shaking in a way that didn't seem to bother him anymore.

'All the best. *Better Homes and Gardens* is on,' he said, checking his watch.

He hobbled back to his armchair. I was ready to bolt out of the room but instead helped him lower himself into his seat. He attempted to bump the orientation of his chair to face his dated television.

'Can I help?' I asked.

'I've got it, I've got it,' he said.

His TV hung on the wall next to a series of silver photo frames. A black and white picture was the feature. It showed two young men with their arms around each other. One had a large hook nose and big cartoonish ears. Leonard had the same features as that young man, yet was somehow even paler than the photo.

'Is that… is that you with Mick Jagger?' I asked.

'Yeah, that's me and Mick.'

Oh sure. First name basis. Mick Jagger was laughing along with a young Leonard, both wearing bright turtleneck sweaters that looked out of place even in that era. The frame next to it had a shot of Leonard being lifted up by The Beach Boys, all grinning with striped shirts and over-brushed hair.

'How do you know all these people?'

'Ah, a past life, young man. A past life.' Leonard appeared to be searching for something in his seat.

In the doorway, one foot was ready to make the exit; the other was still curious enough to keep me in the room.

'You were a musician?'

'Oh yes. I was a singer-songwriter back in the seventies. Ran off to America to make it big,' he said. My insides stung. That was *my* plan, Leonard. Except for the singing and the songwriting. And the seventies. Envy didn't fuss about the details.

His room was populated more by the retirement home furnishings than any personal belongings. Just a desk with some papers and stationery, a desk chair, the armchair, a basic bed and the cheapest wardrobe a retirement home could buy. There were no framed gold albums hanging up. No Grammys occupied the desk. Nothing to mark success in the music industry, just a couple of photos with celebrities and people I didn't recognise that resembled Leonard's family.

'And I did alright, I did,' said Leonard. 'Got to see the world. Ate a lot of doughnuts. It was a good run.'

'How come you didn't stay in America?'

'Oh I went back and forth a lot. But there's no place like Australia. I miss the doughnuts but we have better pies. Meat pies that is. We don't do apple pies like them. Lots of sugar in those pies. But you can't get a meat pie there. And they call sauce ketchup. Did you know that?'

'I did.'

'Funny word. Funny word.'

At this desk, I lifted one of the photo frames towards him. A teenage boy and girl stood at the airport with signs saying, 'Welcome Home Dad!'.

'Your kids?' I asked.

'That's George and Kathy. They're all grown up now. Beautiful families.'

'Leonard can I ask, did you stop doing music because of, you know, wife and kids?'

'God no. My wife was my biggest supporter. The music industry is a tough industry if you don't have the nerve to try. My wife had enough nerve for the both of us.'

'And the kids? Didn't you spend a lot of time away?'

'Sometimes,' he said. 'But having the kids made it all worthwhile.' Leonard found the TV remote that had fallen into the cushion of his armchair and straightened up again.

'I've always been worried that if I had kids my career would be over,' I said, placing the frame back down.

'What's your job?'

'I'm a comedian.'

'A comedian, hey? Well, then are you creative?'

'Um. I guess so, yeah.'

'Well if you're creative you can figure it out. You've got the mind for it.' Leonard showed his deep brown eyes. People say eyes can look wise. I tried to see that in his but they just looked tired.

'Thanks,' I said, picking at my fingernails. 'I needed to hear that.'

'I know a joke actually.'

'Go on.' I smirked.

'There was a bloke who went to the doctor and said, 'Doc, I keep thinking that I'm living in the future.' The doctor said 'That's no good. Why's that?' and the bloke says… oh no wait I've messed it up.'

'That's alright Leonard, I'm sure it was a corker.'

'Anyway, *Better Homes and Gardens* is on.'

He clicked the remote, turning on my signal to leave. Before I left the building, I took a mint from the bowl.

***

The bus smelled of leftover KFC. A box skidded back and forth across the floor each time we turned a corner. None of the other people around me seemed bothered by it. It became a greasy pendulum, lulling me into a hypnotic state. My headphones blocked out the chatting school kids in front of me. They were babies once. As recent as yesterday. Their school bags were filled with their hopes, dreams and empty lunch boxes. I imagined what I'd pack for my son one day. Dunkaroos would be delicious and make for high-value trades. He could get two packets of Tiny Teddies if he could negotiate well and inherit his mother's charm. I'd let him watch cartoons in the morning, so he'd have Pokémon stickers on the lunch box. He'd have a Pikachu keyring on the zipper of his bag. I'd zip it up for him and kiss his forehead.

Pokémon would teach him so much about being a dignified human. It wasn't like Harry Potter, who was told he was the chosen one from day dot. You knew from the first chapter of the first book that Harry is going to defeat evil and win the day. The lead character of Pokémon was Ash, who vowed to be the very best Pokémon trainer of them all. Yet no matter how hard he tried, he couldn't win a tournament. He wasn't the chosen one. He wasn't even a competent one. The story showed that winning isn't as important as 'the friends you make along the way'. Maybe I'd judged the hostel guy too hard for watching Dragon Ball Z as an adult. There were lessons in cartoons we may have missed as kids.

My phone buzzed to tell me I had to get back to the present. It was a message from Jin.

'Hey man, I'm going to need that money back pretty soon. My parents have cut me off since I told them I'm going to do stand-up full time.'

Stand-up was a wild sea. You could thrive in the intense storm of cheers and applause, revel in the travel and then submit to long stretches of struggle. It was late nights and not enough pay to even afford a packet of Dunkaroos. Stand-up comedy was hard and dumb and unsustainable and I was prepared to do it forever if I could.

When I was seven years old, our class was on the school bus being taken to the performance hall to do our grade-two play. The teacher, Miss McDowell, stood at the front in the aisle grumbling about us needing to behave ourselves when we got there. We were to get into our costumes straight away with no messing around. As she delivered this pre-emptive scolding, I stood on the seat behind her and mimed actions to what she was saying, pulling faces and pretending to put on costumes. As the other kids cackled at my impromptu silent theatre, Miss McDowell turned and caught me mid-funny face. There was a moment right before she yelled at me that I could see her suppress a laugh. Just a moment. The corner of her lips curled enough for me to know I had got her. The subsequent reproach was so loud and fierce it scared me into tears in front of the whole bus. I sobbed as Miss McDowell made me apologise to the class for my behaviour. The image of her cracking, however, was mine to keep. That was better than the forced applause we later got for the school play.

If I could make a teacher laugh, then I could make comedy my living. That sentiment stayed into my adulthood, even through all the financial crises. Not paying Jin back for a while was a consideration. Not because I couldn't find a way. If he really wanted to be a comedian he could do it on a can of beans for a while to prove he really wanted it. A pregnancy scare wouldn't hurt either.

'Of course, man. I've got you.' I sent him. There was nothing that noble about beans.

As the city flew by the window into the suburbs, I went back to watching the box of KFC. I wondered if there was anything left in it.

***

I stood in front of a red brick warehouse checking the map on my phone. This was meant to be the DNA lab. It looked like a steel factory from the nineteen-sixties that was battling to keep business alive. Out front there were metal beams lying in a heap. A faded sign reading 'DNA Key Labs' met me in the hallway. I followed the pale green arrow on it to a reception desk, the documents tucked under my arm.

'Hi, I'm here for a paternity test,' I said.

The woman behind the desk didn't break from her computer screen as she stretched out her open hand. I placed the documents in it. She skimmed over them and wrote some notes. They might have been things like 'lol' and 'another deadbeat dad haha'. Her expression couldn't have been colder if it were snowing.

'Head into that room.' She pointed.

'Thank you,' I said. She made a faint smirk and went back to her screen. This place was not going to get a good review from me on TripAdvisor.

The room contained a sagging grey couch and a chipped glass coffee table. I leafed through last year's copy of *Woman's Day*: 'Beyoncé's surrogate mother revealed!'. I skimmed the story, ready to turn the page in case someone walked in and judged me for being interested in such gossip. There had already been enough judgement today.

A man-child in a white lab coat walked in with a small paper box. He had pimples on his forehead and could have been two ten-year-olds, one standing on the other's shoulders. Tall and unstable.

'Okay cool,' he said. 'I just need to take a swab from your cheek.' He revealed a long cotton swab encased in a test tube.

'Sure,' I replied. 'Hey, can you explain the difference between a pre-natal DNA test and this one?'

'I don't really know that stuff.' He wobbled. 'You'd have to ask someone in the lab.'

'I thought we were in the lab.'

Unclipping the swab was his only interest.

'Open your mouth.' He scraped the brush along the inside of my cheek then returned it to the tube. 'One more.' He repeated the process with another. He signed both tubes and got me to do the same. I'd practised my autograph a lot over the years but the bend of the tube made it hard to do it to the Hollywood standard I aspired to.

'That's it,' he said and shuffled out. I was left in the room with the *Woman's Day*. I finished the gossip story before having the clarity of mind to leave.

At reception I asked when the results would come through.

'Monday. You'll get an email,' the receptionist said.

'Is there any way to get it sooner?'

'No.' She didn't seem busy enough to be rude. Perhaps it had been a bad day for her. Maybe she didn't even work here. She might just be some random off the street who came in to do her own paternity test. There might be any number of reasons for her attitude but I wouldn't let them get in the way of my occupation.

'Okay,' I said. 'Just try not to accidentally switch the sample with a lab rat.'

She pushed her lips into a smile then looked back at her computer. At least I tried.

26

AT 8:59 A.M., I called the DNA lab.

'What's your name?' the receptionist asked.

'Ben Thomas.'

'Do you have the ID number there?'

'Yes, 846871-PL.'

'Okay, I can see it here. The lab will send the results via email at some time this morning.'

'Can I not get them sooner?'

'I'm afraid not.'

I bit my bottom lip but released it to take a deep breath.

'Thank you,' I said. For nothing.

In the days since the birth, Tash had only sent one message; she was exhausted and her parents were with her and the baby. I responded with six, or twenty, messages of support, questions and hopeful sentiments. Jin and Libby had both expressed surprise at the news of the birth, Libby because she recognised the kid was premature and Jin because he assumed I'd be in LA by now. Their questions for me went unanswered as mine did with Tash. They'd know what was happening with my American job when I did. There was some knowledge only a legitimate father was privy to. It was too soon to tell Dad anything. He got sad at losing a plant, let alone the idea of being a grandfather.

The tattooed New Zealander was snoring on the bunk above me. His inked arm was dangling off the side, taunting me to tug it. I swung my head around it, getting to my feet, finding my shoes and hopping around the obstacle course of belongings to leave the dorm.

In the rec room, there were half a dozen wrinkled beanbags on the carpet in front of the television. It was playing a rerun of *Everyone Loves Raymond*. I dropped onto one of the bags. There was a Japanese guy nearby playing a Nintendo Switch. I watched the episode of Raymond while checking my phone every half-second. Even without paying full attention, the core dilemma in the show for Raymond seemed different to me now. The real tension of the show was for Raymond to decide between the person that he had to love, his mother, and the person that he chose to love, his wife. Food and sex now seemed so primitive.

The room felt hot and stuffy and suffocating and excruciating. Hopping off the beanbag, I escaped the hostel. My heart was trying to remember how to start a panic attack. I slowed my breathing and remembered what Zack had told me. *This can't kill me. It's just fear. Breathe. Deep breath.* When that didn't work, I ran.

Through the city, I bolted over the stone tiles that made up the footpaths and darted across the roads without waiting for a green man. There was a narrow miss with a man attending to his phone. A past me, perhaps. The main street veered towards a greener patch and fewer potential collisions. No more hospitals, please.

My shoes hit the grass at Kings Park and led me up the hill. My lungs stung from the shock activity and a stitch appeared to join the party. At the top of the hill my body decided it needed to crumble forward onto a park bench to interrogate what part of me thought I was fit enough to do this. My panting soon eased into regular breathing and my heart forgot if it was panicking or exercising. It gave up deciding and slowly returned to normal.

The tops of green trees caressed the view of the blue and white buildings of the city centre. The Swan River stretched out flat and relaxed. It offered a reflection of a Cessna flying over it. What a place to have problems.

As the breeze cooled me down, I just wanted to hold that child, to see him giggle and babble, to tickle the chubby rolls of skin around his soft pink neck, to calm his cries and help him find sleep. When I was growing up I had never understood why my Dad would always check on me while I was sleeping, tuck me in extra tight, buy me knee and elbow pads when I wanted to skateboard and pick me up from every single party when I was a teenager. I got it now. Whatever had lay dormant inside me was now awake and ready to climb another hill to care for that sweet boy.

My phone pinged.

The screen unlocked to show a mini red '1' above the email icon. There was no more breathing despite the plea from my lungs. My throat was held shut by an invisible fist, tight and unrelenting.

The subject line of the email read: 'DNA Test Report: 846871-PL'.

I hadn't eaten since last night but whatever was in my gut was ready to make its way down the side of the hill. My heart threw punches at my chest like it wanted to burst out and read the email for itself. The pounding shuddered through me while the rest of the world went quiet.

Based on the results of the DNA parentage testing, it can be seen that Ben Thomas is excluded from identification as the father of Luke Peters.

Tears.

I fought my chest for shallow breaths between the hard sobs. My hands covered my face and I cried until my whole body was sore.

27

I COLLECTED MY BACKPACK from the dorm and left the hostel without asking for a refund for my remaining stay. It was no place for my kind. Sex in a dorm was to be expected but crying would be just rude.

Down James Street, I cut through the park to avoid the noise of traffic and place another call to Tash. There was no ringtone at all. Straight to voicemail. At a park bench, I tried to keep my fingers steady while sending the fifth text in the last half an hour. There was no activity on her social media pages. An anomaly for our generation.

Wandering the streets became hazardous. A haze of thought dulled the hum of car engines. Crossing roads didn't get my full attention. Years of waiting for a response from Tash squeezed themselves into minutes. An upsetting thought leaked from my brain into the rest of my body. Maybe she had blocked my number.

Why would she do that? Why to holy fuck would she do that?

A map search revealed a nearby payphone. Inside, I scooped out all the coins my backpack contained and fed them into the slot. The phone earpiece was broken on one side, displaying a tangle of coloured wires.

My finger stabbed into the dial with Tash's number.

It rang.

'Hello?' Her voice was timid and unsure.

'Tash it's Ben. I just wanted to…'

The line went dead. The streets began to spiral around me. The phone left my hand. I paced around the outside of the booth, tugging at my hair until the next plan emerged.

I called an Uber.

***

It wasn't until the sun was setting that the ute pulled up over the curb and parked along the tyre marks on the front lawn. The footballer stepped out, wearing a fluro yellow work top, shorts and Blundstone boots. He had a five o'clock shadow that beat anything I could grow in a week. He slammed the door shut and went around the back to pull out tools from the tray.

Crossing the road, my knees were unsure they could take the weight of what I was doing.

'Hey!' I said, feeling my cheeks run hot with blood.

His head snapped in my direction.

'What the fuck?' He grimaced and turned his whole body now, his chest puffed and arms tensing.

'Listen, just listen,' I said, my palms held out at him. I was on his side of the street but didn't step up from the gutter. 'This is super important and urgent. I don't know if you know but Tash had…' I couldn't get anything else out. A crack in my throat broke open to a rush of more sobs. My fingers pressed into my eyes. I didn't see the footballer before I felt his hand on me.

'Mate, calm down.' He kept a hand on my shoulder but his arm was outstretched.

Enough air came to me to keep talking.

'Tash had the baby and it's not mine.' Again my throat succumbed to emotion before it could get any more words out.

'I told you it can't be mine, mate.' Blood shot into his face. 'First off, it's none of your fucking business. And I told you I wore a condom.'

He gave me a moment to respond but I didn't. 'Look,' he said. 'I don't want to have to call the cops but you got to stop coming here.'

My whole jaw was quivering. I looked down the street at nothing, letting the flood of feelings drain out enough to generate a thought. It took far too long. The footballer was a stone wall I didn't have the strength or tools to break. Jokes could only break so much tension.

'You better go,' he said and strode back to the house.

'Hey!' I yelled louder than the distance required. The strange, heavy-built man swung his body around once more. He stood alone like me, away from a family he didn't want and I now couldn't have. His muscle and stubbornness would shield him from his life mistakes. He may never have to do more than walk away from anything.

'Talk to her. Please. Just talk to her,' I said.

He went inside without turning back.

28

'WHEN I WAS A KID, I always wanted to be a basketballer.' My height was enough to make the audience chuckle. 'Hey don't laugh. I'm five-seven. When I round it up two inches.' This got them going even more.

'For real, though. I wanted to be a full-time, professional NBA basketball player. I had the basketball shorts and the singlet with the ventilation holes in it. Pretty sure that was for aerodynamics. That's what they were for right? I had the pump-up shoes that made you run faster just because you were eight-years-old and didn't understand how science works.'

A guy in a Lakers cap two tables away clapped and laughed in recognition with more gusto than the rest of the room.

'This guy!' I pointed him out. 'This guy is all grown up and still wearing that shit.' The crowd filled the room with a warmth that only laughter or an industrial size heater could make. The bright orange sign behind me bore the Laugh Factory logo, the backdrop to so many videos of my favourite comedians. They always filmed the sets of the comics here just in case magic happened. Perhaps that helped comedians believe it would.

'You remember those pump shoes right, dude? Two pumps of the tongue and you acted like it would change the game.' I mimed pumping the shoes. 'Time to change the scores, baby!' I couldn't help but chuckle along too.

'I practised my basketball skills every day: dribbling, layups, my three-pointer shot, high fiving teammates. Most importantly I practised how to spin the ball on my finger, which is useful when you are demonstrating how planets work during the game. Sport is important but physics is for the real cool kids.' That one lost some of the crowd but it hit enough funny bones to stay in the act.

'I played ball for my school team and a local team, because that would double my chances of being discovered by the NBA... in the northern suburbs of Melbourne. You know, where all the talent scouts are.

'Then I hit about thirteen years old and all of a sudden everyone else playing was taller than me. I was useless to the team. I went from point guard to a Make-a-Wish Kid like that.' I clicked. The crowd burst into a violent laugh, then about half of them made a guilty groan.

'Oh no, don't you groan at that after you definitely laughed,' I chortled. 'If you started with a laugh then you're going to hell as much as the rest of us. You don't get to go to heaven and say, "Yes God, I laughed at the Make-a-Wish Kid joke at first but then I groaned." You can't expect God will be like "Ah well that's fine, come on through!"'

I danced backwards like a jester welcoming guests into the court. The giggles kept me prancing around until they died out and I perched on the stool that lived on stage. It was made of wood but felt like a giant cushion in that moment. My shoulders relaxed and my face split into a grin.

'So anyway,' I was still giggling too. The heaven joke wasn't planned so it surprised me as much as the crowd. 'One day, I come home crying and I tell my dad I'm not going to play basketball anymore. He shrugs and says, "Yeah that makes sense." I say, "What do you mean that makes sense?" He says, "Everyone in the family is short, so this was always going to happen."

'What!? Why did he lie to me for so many years!? He told me I could achieve anything I set my mind to!'

The Lakers cap was rocking back and forth, laughing and snorting.

'Do you still play ball, man?' I asked him.

'Nah, I gave up.' The whole room cackled, including me.

'Thank you! We can relate. What do you do now?'

'I work in sales,' he said.

'There you go, boring as hell. I think the moral of the story here is follow your achievable dreams.' The audience applauded. I rode it like a wave into the next line.

'See I had this imagined life.' My bum shuffled back to be square on the seat. 'I was going to grow up, join the NBA, play for the best team, win trophies, buy a mansion, have a dog, get a wife, have kids and they would be NBA champions as well. The day I realised I couldn't compete in basketball anymore was the day my imagined life died. And grief for an imagined life is as real as any other grief.'

There was a quiet confusion. I'd broken the rhythm. Even if you watched comedy in a language you didn't understand, there was still a drumbeat of laughter you could follow. The comic was just a percussionist, with lines instead of sticks and crowds instead of kits.

'It took me a long time to get over that grief. But after a while, I held my chin up, accepted that I'm a short-arse, looked in the mirror and said to myself…'

The tension held. During my years at the Exford Hotel, silence was the enemy. Back then, it was the absence of joy. It had crawled under my skin and made me want to scratch it out. But now, it could be wielded with confidence. Under my control, the silence could hold a room in place so that I could deliver the final punchline.

'*Whelp! If this is as tall as I'm going to get, I better get fucking funny.*'

The crowd roared as the line landed. The mic clipped back onto the stand with a squeeze of my fingers. I said goodbye to the three hundred strangers beyond the bright lights with a raise of my hand.

'I've been Ben Thomas, goodnight Los Angeles!'

I leave the stage, immersed in cheers. The MC high-fives me as I slip past. He tells the audience to keep it going for me. At the club's entrance, the bouncer holds the door open and says he'll see me again next week. Sunset Boulevard is bright and alive. Headlights are darting past me in each direction. People are strutting, dressed up for the nightlife. I button up my corduroy jacket, then find my car under the silhouette of a palm tree. The doors unlock at the press of my key fob.

The engine starts and I click the heat dial up. California is as close to cold as it ever is around this time. I recline in the driver's seat, tapping at my phone. After a few minutes of zombie scrolling through Instagram, I type Tash's name into the search bar. Nothing comes up. I log out of my account. I create a new profile with a different email and do the search again. Natasha Peters is there. Her account is set to private but the profile photo is visible now. A long-haired Tash hugs a five-year-old boy.

It's his birthday today.

ACKNOWLEDGEMENTS

Thanks to my editor Lu Sexton for not letting me get away with lazy writing, even though it would have allowed me to retain my hair colour.

To Larrikin House for asking me to write this story. I hope it makes you a bazillion dollars.

Olivia Petzy and Richard Binning for letting me sleep on your couch when the real ordeal took placc. I hope you giggled at your cameos.

Dr Brad McKay, who explained how ultrasounds work when I most needed to know.

To all the room bookers, venues, fellow comedians and the rest of the comedy industry, I love you like family: begrudgingly.

Special thanks to Benjamin Stevenson, Matthew Ziccone, Lucy Maddox, Claire Gawne and Mick Neven for reading early drafts. You no doubt saved me from a bunch of disgruntled reviews. I'll hold you responsible for any I do get.

And to my agent Aaron Laing, have the royalties come in yet?